46

F SCO
Scott, Bradford, 1893-1975.
 Frontier doctor

FRONTIER DOCTOR

Tom Carson was beginning to consider himself a failure as a doctor until he got a case that tried his skill and earned him a fat fee. But as an aftermath, he found himself under suspicion and there was only one man who could clear his name, but that was Jim Hill and he was a black sheep, a treacherous outlaw!

Carson's quest for Jim Hill led him to Tombstone in Arizona where he was befriended by Wyatt and Vergil Earp and he earned respect for his skill as a surgeon. But Tombstone quickly changed from a boom city into a ghost town, and amid death and destruction Tom began to win respect for his skills with his heavy guns too.

Bradford Scott was a pseudonym for **Leslie Scott** who was born in Lewisburg, West Virginia. During the Great War, he joined the French Foreign Legion and spent four years in the trenches. In the 1920s he worked as a mining engineer and bridge builder in the western American states and in China before settling in New York. A bar-room discussion in 1934 with Leo Margulies, who was managing editor for Standard Magazines, prompted Scott to try writing fiction. He went on to create two of the most notable series characters in Western pulp magazines. In 1936, Standard Magazines launched, and in *Texas Rangers*, Scott under the house name of **Jackson Cole** created Jim Hatfield, Texas Ranger, a character whose popularity was so great with readers that this magazine featuring his adventures lasted until 1958. When others eventually began contributing Jim Hatfield stories, Scott created another Texas Ranger hero, Walt Slade, better known as *El Halcon*, the Hawk, whose exploits were regularly featured in *Thrilling Western*. In the 1950s Scott moved quickly into writing book-length adventures about both Jim Hatfield and Walt Slade in long series of original paperback Westerns. At the same time, however, Scott was also doing some of his best work in hardcover Westerns published by Arcadia House; thoughtful, well-constructed stories, with engaging characters and authentic settings and situations. Among the best of these, surely, are *Silver City* (1953), *Longhorn Empire* (1954), *The Trail Builders* (1956), and *Blood on the Rio Grande* (1959). In these hardcover Westerns, many of which have never been reprinted, Scott proved himself highly capable of writing traditional Western stories with characters who have sufficient depth to change in the course of the narrative and with a degree of authenticity and historical accuracy absent from many of his series stories.

FRONTIER DOCTOR

Bradford Scott

GUNSMOKE

First published by Quality Press.

This hardback edition 2004
by BBC Audiobooks Ltd
by arrangement with
Golden West Literary Agency

ISBN 1 4056 8001 6

British Library Cataloguing in Publication Data available.

Printed and bound in Great Britain by
Antony Rowe Ltd., Chippenham, Wiltshire

Chapter 1

DOCTOR TOM CARSON sat in his office and fingered a manila rope. His grey eyes were dreamy and anybody observing him would doubtless have concluded that Dr. Carson was pondering some abstruse problem of medical research, or perhaps assembling the details of an intricate surgical operation.

But in fact, Doctor Carson was thinking of roomy ranchhouse kitchens with scrubbed-clean wooden tables groaning under pots of steaming coffee, pans of hot biscuits and platters of sizzling steaks.

That is why he meditatively fingered the supple rope that showed signs of considerable usage.

The fact of the matter being Tom Carson liked to eat.

Being a doctor with a brand new diploma from a well known school of medicine carried prestige and the respect of the community; but up to the present, Carson ruefully admitted that prestige and respect were about all it carried; and prestige and respect, while being very well in their way, did little to tighten the belt.

Folks in Poce and the surrounding section were disgustingly healthy; and those who did happen to suffer from ailments or accidents preferred to travel to Tombstone, the silver town twenty miles to the southwest, where there were practitioners of experience and repute.

About the only practice Carson had been able to glean was patching up bullet holes and knife cuts that were serious enough to demand immediate attention. And while Poce was a pretty warm cowtown, these had not been numerous enough to afford an income sufficient for his needs.

The only case he had had that carried a really ample fee was that of the Poce Bank cashier, who had been drilled through and through in the course of a robbery thought to have been pulled by John Ringold and his outlaw band two weeks previous. The bank had lost a good many thousands of dollars, one clerk had been killed and the cashier seriously wounded.

Folks agreed that Carson saved the life of the cashier by a speedy and efficient operation. The cashier had been grateful and had paid accordingly.

But one good fee now and then is not sufficient to eat on indefinitely. And that was why Tom Carson fingered the twine with which he had roped many a cow before going to college and—at least that's what the diploma said—becoming a doctor.

" Better to twirl a rope and eat regularly than to sit all day in an office and go hungry," he told himself.

But even as he said it, his jaw set grimly and there was a light in his steady grey eyes. Tom Carson didn't take kindly to packing a licking.

It was a grey and dreary afternoon. Low lying clouds, like drifting smoke, hurried across the sky, and from them dripped icy rain, that drove in sheets before a wailing wind. Already, early as was the hour, the windows of the cow town were changing from dark, staring eyes to squares and rectangles of gold as lamps were lighted.

A dejected looking horse, swathed in a blanket, stood at a hitchrack. A bedraggled rooster, tail feathers hanging limp and dripping, essayed a crow, ended it in a disgusted squawk and scurried under a porch. Only a hardened duck appeared unaffected by the general depression and quacked cheerfully as he fished in a pool with an anticipatory bill.

To the east towered the yellow, shadowy ramparts of the Dragoon Mountains, their grim wall seeming almost to overhang the little cow town. To the southwest loomed the gaunt, unlovely Tombstone Hills, their brown slopes, a dreary monotony of boulders and huge rocks, softened by the rain mists, their drab pauper's mantle hiding one of the continent's richest treasures. Farther south were the Huachuca's and to the east, unseen, were the blue, mysterious

Chiricahuas, the grim gateway to Galeyville, capital of Curly Bill Graham's outlaw kingdom.

Abruptly the drear loneliness of the street was broken by a big bay horse churning his way through the mud, from the east. His rider hunched low in the saddle, water streaming from his slicker. Carson got a flickering glimpse of him through the rain streaked window as he flashed past.

But almost instantly the sucking hoofbeats ceased. There was a creaking of wet saddle leather, a jingling of bit irons. Then the solid thud of boots ascending the three steps that led to Carson's little office.

The door banged open and a bulky, black-bearded man stepped in, dashing the water from his hatbrim. He glanced questioningly about the office. His glittering black eyes rested on Carson and held.

"You the doctor?" he asked. His voice was the harsh, unmusical growl of a beast of prey.

Carson nodded.

"Feller out in the brush bad hurt," the man pursued.

"What's the matter with him?" Carson asked.

"Shot cleanin' his gun and it went off."

"Shot where?"

The man tapped his breast just below the heart.

"Right here," he said. "Slug didn't go all the way through."

"What calibre gun?" Carson asked.

"Forty-five," the other growled. "What difference does that make?"

"Plenty," Carson answered. "Funny, a forty-five slug fired at close range usually goes right through a man."

"Well, this one didn't go through," the informant grunted surlily. "It's somewhere inside him."

"Which sounds like it must have struck a bone," Carson commented. "In that case he is bad hurt."

"He looks it," the other said. "Looks like a dead man, but he's still breathin', or was when I saw him last. Will yuh come out and see what yuh can do for him?"

Carson stood up, his lean, sinewy six-foot-two towering over his bulky visitor, who was himself no short man.

" That's a doctor's business, I reckon," he admitted.

From a cabinet he began assembling medicines and instruments, which he placed in a small black case. He snapped the case shut and turned to the man, who was waiting in stolid silence.

" Why didn't yuh bring him here? " he asked.

" Scairt to move him," the other replied. " Scairt it would kill him."

Carson nodded. " Chances are yuh were right," he admitted. " Let's go; I'll have the rig on my horse pronto."

He paused to take his gun belts from a drawer and buckle them on. His visitor eyed the operation curiously.

" Fust time I ever rec'lect seein' a two-gun doctor," he commented.

Carson grinned, his teeth flashing startlingly white and even in his bronzed face.

" Well, I wore 'em so many years I sorta feel undressed without 'em," he explained, almost apologetically.

The visitor grunted, but proffered no further comment.

A few minutes later, Carson and the stocky black-eyed man rode eastward through the gathering shadows. Beyond the last straggle of the town, the man turned his horse's head to the northeast.

For several miles he pursued this course, then abruptly turned his horse due east into the mouth of a shadowy canyon. Another mile of a rough and winding trail that was little more than a game track and the man pulled up. He fished a black handkerchief from his pocket and dangled it in his left hand.

" Reckon we'll put this over yore eyes from here on, Doc." he said.

Tom Carson stared at him, his grey eyes narrowing a trifle.

" Reckon we'll not," he announced with decision.

The man's face darkened. " I say yuh will, and that's what I mean," he growled.

At the same instant his right hand flashed to the heavy gun sagging on his hip.

But Tom Carson's slim hand also flashed down, and up. There was the crash of a report, echoing dully between the rock walls of the canyon.

The bearded man yelled—a shrill, crackling yell of rage and pain. He dropped the handkerchief and pawed at his blood spurting right hand. His gun, the lock smashed by the heavy slug from Carson's Colt, lay in the mud of the trail.

Tom Carson spoke through the wisping smoke of his gun.

"If yuh'd hand yore holster a little more to the front, and *not* tie it down, mebbe yuh could unleather yore iron with a little more speed than a snail climbing a slick log," he said, his voice low and quiet, but with a note in it like to the grind of steel on ice.

The bearded man cursed insanely, his eyes points of black fire in his livid face. Carson regarded him coolly with a level grey gaze.

"Reckon I'll take yuh to Tombstone and turn yuh over to Sherriff Behan," he remarked, "I've a notion he'd be plumb glad to see yuh."

The man quieted instantly, his eyes intent on Carson's bleak face.

"I ain't scairt of Johnny Behan—ain't done nothin' to be scairt of," he growled; "but if yuh do that, I reckon the kid that's shot will hafta cash in his chips, if he ain't done it already."

Carson eyed the man. There was a ring of sincerity in his voice. Undoubtedly despite the sudden apparently inexplicable turn of events, there was a man somewhere in the hills who desperately needed the services of a doctor. Carson suddenly remembered the words of the old dean of medicine, wise in the ways of men and the world, mellowed and understanding by a long life of service.

"A doctor's mission is to save life and alleviate suffering," the dean had said. "No circumstance relieves him of that duty. Personal preference or convenience must never be allowed to stand in the way. He dedicates his life to the service of humanity, and in that service he must never be found wanting."

Carson nodded his head, as if the venerable speaker had been standing before him.

"Go on, lead the way," he told the bearded man. "This is a damn funny affair, but I'll do what I can for that feller who's shot."

The man stared at him unbelievingly. He hesitated.

"I was told to bring yuh blindfolded," he mumbled.

"Listen," Carson told him. "I understand the business. Yuh're one of a band of owlhoots hiding out here in the hills. The feller who's shot is another member. Okay. I'm not a sheriff or peace officer of any kind. It's not my business to run down outlaws. It is my business to help folks who are sick or hurt, no matter who they are or what they are. I know, too, that where yuh're taking me is not yore outfit's head-quarters—yuh'd never have that so close to town. Where you were ordered to bring me is just a temporary hangout that yuh'll trail away from as soon as it's practicable to do so. After I've treated that man, and got him in shape to move—and if I work on him, I can't leave him till he is able to move—yuh'll pull out, and if I brought somebody back here looking for yuh, none of you would be here."

"Reckon yuh've sorta called the turn," the man admitted grudgingly. "All right. I'm liable to catch hell from the Boss for doing it, but I'm gonna take a chance. Let's go."

"Wait a minute," Carson delayed. 'I'll bandage yore hand first—it's bleeding badly."

His attention called back to his hand, the man cursed venomously; but he permitted Carson to treat the deep furrow across the back of his hand and put it in a bandage. He glanced ruefully at his shattered gun.

"That was my pet shootin' iron, and yuh done busted it all to hell," he growled.

"Before yuh get another one to pack, yuh better learn to handle it," Carson advised dryly.

The man shot him a venomous glance, that nevertheless was tinged with grudging admiration.

" If I didn't know different, after seein' that draw of yores, I'd be willing to swear yuh're Buckskin Frank Leslie and nobody else," he declared. " Yuh'd make Doc Holliday or Curly Bill Graham look silly. If yuh can handle a doctor's tools like yuh can a gun, mebbe the kid won't hafta take the big jump, after all, if he ain't took it already. Come on! "

Turning his horse, he headed directly for the north wall of the canyon. As they drew near, Carson glanced up the beetling precipice.

" Well if yuh figger to go up that, yuh must aim to sprout wings," he remarked.

" You'll see," grunted the outlaw.

However, it was not until they were within a few yards of the lofty wall that Carson " saw."

Suddenly from the black wall started a man holding a cocked rifle at the ready and peering at the approaching horsemen with out-thrust neck; for now the gloom was thick.

Suddenly he stood before them, as a ghost might do, though whence he came, Carson could not at the moment see. In another moment, however, the mystery was explained. Carson saw that in the cliff face was a narrow cleft, invisible from but a few paces away, since its outer edge projected over the the inner wall of rock.

" That you, Hill? " the man called hoarsely.

" Yeah, its me," Carson's companion answered. " I got the Doc with me. Has Billy cashed in yet? "

" Nope," the other replied as he stood aside to make way for them. " He's still breathin', but he looks mighty bad. Yuh better hustle if yuh want to do anythin' for him."

With the rifleman trailing behind them, Carson and the man called Hill threaded their way through the cleft. Inside the crevice it was almost black dark, for the rock walls were so lofty that but a narrow thread of gloomy sky was to be seen above, and from it little light filtered to the depths.

For several hundred yards they pursued the dreary, winding

path. At length the cleft widened somewhat and the light grew stronger. Abruptly they found themselves on a little plateau in the mountainside. Hill turned to the left and a moment later drew rein in front of a cave mouth in the cliff, from which struggled a gleam of ruddy light.

"Light off, Doc," he directed hoarsely. "Jack will look after yore horse. Don't worry about him; he'll be waitin' for yuh when yuh're ready to trail yore rope."

Carson dismounted, and Hill led the way into the cave. It curved sharply a few yards from the entrance. Rounding the bend, Carson paused, blinking in the glare of light from a fire and several lanterns hung along the rock wall.

Lounging about the fire were nearly a dozen men who glanced up questioningly.

One stepped forward, a tall, darkly handsome man of sculpturesque physique and lean, saturnine face. Carson recognized him at once. It was John Ringo, Curly Bill Graham's chief lieutenant, and thought by many to be the brains of Curly Bill's gang.

Ringo spoke, his voice low pitched and musical.

"Thought I told you to bring him blindfolded, Hill?" he said.

"Yeah, I know yuh did," Hill replied, with a venomous glance at Carson; "but he sorta didn't see it that way."

He held up his bandaged hand significantly as he spoke.

"I need a gun," he added. "This hellion sorta spiled mine."

Ringo let his sombre eyes rest on Carson's face.

"Why'd you come if you didn't have to?" he asked.

"I understand there's somebody here who badly needs a doctor's attention," Carson replied. "That's why."

Ringo nodded. "Guess I can understand that," he admitted. "Okay—here's your patient."

He turned and led the way to the far side of the cave. On a rough bunk of blankets lay a man. A boy, rather, for Carson instantly saw that he could hardly be more than eighteen years old. He saw also that the patient was near death. His face was colourless, his lips grey. He breathed in stertorous gasps and his long-lashed eyelids rested on his waxen cheeks.

"Well?" asked Ringo.

Carson's answer was to begin cutting away the rough bandage that swathed the boy's chest. His black brows drew together as he laid bare the bullet wound a couple of inches below the heart.

"Yuh say the slug is still in there?" he asked Ringo.

"That's right," the outlaw chief replied. "Was cleaning his gun and it went off."

"His arms must be a heap sight longer than they look, or mebbe they stretch," Carson replied dryly.

"Mebbe," Ringo said, a ghost of a smile flitting across his dark face. He evidently comprehended the significance of Carson's remark.

Carson drew a stethoscope from his bag and applied it to the wounded man's chest. His brows knit as he listened. A moment later he stood up and faced Ringo, who looked at him questiongly.

"From the sound, I'd say the slug is lying alongside the aorta, the great trunk artery that carries blood from the heart to be distributed by branch arteries through the body," Carson said. "It must be pressing against the aorta. Perhaps it slightly ruptured the wall. The pulse of the artery keeps rubbing the wall against the bullet—it has already thinned the wall to some extent, judging from the sound of the rush of arterial blood."

"Which means he'll die?"

"That remains to be seen," Carson replied. "If the bullet is allowed to remain, he certainly will die, when the rupture of the wall of the blood vessel is completed."

"Sort of blow up inside," Ringo commented.

"Something like that," Carson agreed, "There will instantly be a massive hæmorrhage, which of course will be fatal."

"Anything to do about it?"

"I can operate," Carson replied quietly. "It may kill him—likely as not it will, but if the slug is not removed, he's going to take the big jump sure for certain."

Ringo's reaction was hairtrigger.

" Go ahead and operate," he said. " What do you want us to do?"

" Make hot water—all yuh can," Carson instructed. " Move all those lanterns and place them around and above the bunk. I'll need all the light I can get—there won't be enough as it is. You'll have to be anæsthetist and handle the chloroform."

" He's utterly unconscious as it is," Ringo commented.

" Yes, but when I begin to cut he might not stay that way," Carson replied. " One move at the wrong time would be fatal. I'm going to give him a heart stimulant now; his heart will need everything it's got, and more besides. It's risky, for any added heart activity tends to increase the pressure of the slug on the artery wall, but I've got to chance it."

He measured the minute dose of the powerful drug with the utmost nicety, charged the hypodermic and injected it. For some minutes he stood watching the patient, while the outlaws busied themselves with the needful preparations. Carson nodded with satisfaction as a faint tinge of colour appeared in the wan cheeks and some of the deathly grey left the boy's lips.

" All right," he told Ringo, " here is the chloroform. Now do exactly as I tell yuh."

The sombre outlaw chief obeyed instructions implicitly. His hand did not shake and his chiselled features did not change expression as Carson began to use the knife. A few moments later Carson removed a section of splintered rib. Another moment and he uttered a low exclamation.

" I can see it, now,—" he told Ringo. " Lying right where I thought it would be. Another minute and the chore's done—or he's done for."

He bent low over the heaving chest, while Hill held a lantern close with a hand that shook a trifle.

Carson straightened up. Between his fingers was a battered bit of lead. The unconscious man's chest still heaved.

With swift, sure hands, Carson closed and dressed the incision. Again he straightened up.

" I believe he'll pull through," he said.

The dead silence of the cave was broken by a sighing sound as every man there exhaled the breath he had been holding.

" God!" muttered a burly, thickset individual, " that was harder to take than seein' the other jigger clear leather fust in a handkerchief duel!"

Chapter 2

CARSON began cleaning and replacing his instruments. Ringo watched him gravely.

" You'll be leaving now, Doc? " he asked.

" Hell, no! " Carson replied. I can't leave a patient in the shape he's in. I'll hafta stick around until I know the outcome of the operation. He's a long way from being out of danger yet."

" How long? " the outlaw chief asked.

" A week at least, mebbe more," Carson said.

Ringo nodded. He turned to his men.

" Ike, you and Hill will stay here with me," he directed. " The rest of you trail your ropes, and scatter. Get going."

The order was instantly obeyed. A few minutes later hoofbeats drew away from the cave. Hill and the thickset burly man remained with Ringo. The burly man, Carson learned, was Ike Clanton, the wounded boy's brother.

Billy Clanton was conscious the following morning, though very weak. He was a likeable boy; but Carson sensed a deadliness about him comparable to that of his older brother and the sullen, taciturn Hill.

John Ringo was different from his companions. He spoke a different language. His speech was not the careless diction of the Southwest and Carson quickly decided that he was undoubtedly a man of some education and breeding; a man born for better things, who, having thrown his life recklessly away, drowned his memories in cards and drink and wild deeds. Carson wondered if it really had been Ringo and his band who robbed the Poce bank, murdered the clerk and wounded the cashier. All the robbers who took part in the foray had been masked. They rode horses bearing practically unreadable Mexican brands. There were folks who thought

16

the tall leader of the raiders was Ringo, but they had little on which to base their suspicion.

That Ringo was a member of Curly Bill's band was well known.   Carson knew, also, that he and the Clantons and the McLowery's often showed up in Tombstone.   Sheriff Johnny Behan was tolerant of them, if not on downright friendly terms, and did not molest them.   Virgil Earp, marshal of Tombstone, considered them the sheriff's problem and let them alone so long as they conducted themselves quietly while in town.   Many stories were told of their depredations, but proof that would stand up in a court of law was not forthcoming, as yet.

Seven days passed before Carson decided that Billy Clanton was out of danger and could be moved.   He told Ringo so.

" Okay, Doc," Ringo replied.   " Reckon you'll be trailing your rope now.   Here."

He drew from his pocket a thick packet of bills and handed them to Carson.

But Tom Carson made no move to take the bundle.   Instead, he looked the owlhoot chief straight in the eye.

" I can't take that money, Ringo," he said quietly.

" Why not? " asked Ringo.

" I reckon you know why without me telling yuh," Carson replied.   " Besides, that's a heap more than I'd have any right to charge."

Ringo slowly nodded, and replaced the money in his pocket.

" Yes, I guess I know why," he replied to Carson's first statement.   " I'm sorry, Doc, but that's the only kind of money I've got."

" Forget it," Carson told him.   " Saving a man's life is something."

Again Ringo nodded.   He spoke, his deep voice tinged with bitterness.

" Perhaps some day I'll get some honest money, and then I won't forget you," he said.

"Okay," agreed Carson, " we'll let it go at that.   Will yuh get my horse for me?   I'll be riding then."

B

"Right," nodded Ringo. "Come on, Ike, and we'll get the Doc's horse from the corral."

Together the two men left the cave, leaving only Hill and Billy Clanton, who was sleeping, with Carson.

Hill darted a quick glance at the sleeping man.

"Doc," he said in low tones, "just how much would yore charge come to?"

"Everything considered, I figure a hundred dollars would be just about right. Why?" Carson replied courteously.

"Here's why," said Hill. He fumbled something from his pocket. It was a greasy hundred-dollar bill, quite different in appearance from the crisp notes Ringo had offered Carson.

"Doc," Hill said earnestly, "I reckon yuh've guessed that Billy Clanton is my bunky. I ain't forgot—won't ever forget—what yuh did for him. This here money is honest money. I worked for it, a long time back. I've carried this bill as a sorta backlog in case I'd need some dinero in a hurry. Yuh know how it is with us fellers. We drink and gamble away everything we get our hands on mighty fast. That's why I held onto this hundred against a time when I'd have real use for it. I figger that time's come. Here—take it."

Carson hesitated. But he desperately needed the money, and there was a ring of sincerity in Hill's voice. He took the bill the owlhoot forced into his hand.

"Don't tell the boss anything about it," cautioned Hill. "They'd figger I'd been holding out on 'em. We don't trust each other very much."

Carson could well believe that, and nodded his understanding as he stowed the money away. Outside sounded a clatter of hoofs and Ringo's shout. With a word of thanks to Hill, he left the cave. The tall outlaw's sullen eyes gleamed exultantly as Carson passed from view. With a muttered curse he examined the healing wound on his gun hand.

Outside the cave, Carson said good-bye to Ringo, mounted his horse and rode into the narrow crevice. Where the crevice debouched into the outer canyon, Carson reined in a moment and studied the terrain. He knew that, with his plainsman's instinct for distance and direction, he could easily find the cave again.

Not that he had any intention of doing so. It was sure for certain that the outlaws would immediately trail their ropes. Also, his visit to their hangout being in the capacity of a doctor, he was under no obligation to reveal the position of the hangout to the county authorities, even had there been any particular reason for doing so. Ringo and his companions might bear the reputation of outlaws, but just the fact that they were sojourning in a cave in the mountains at the moment was no proof that they were hiding from the law. All had maintained that young Billy Clanton had accidentally shot himself while cleaning his gun. Under such circumstances, with the boy dangerously wounded, it was perfectly logical that they should seek out some place where he could be sheltered and cared for. The incident of the blindfold was significant, but not final. Nor was Ringo's tacit admission that the money he offered Carson was not " honest" money.

For, as Carson understood perfectly, " honesty " in the frontier country was largely gradated to the personal conception of the individual. There was no doubt that Graham's gang ran cows across the Line from Mexico; also, they engaged to some extent in smuggling, and preyed on other smuggling bands. These things, while outside the strict letter of the law, were looked upon complacently along the frontier. Many a prosperous and respected cattle baron got his start lifting cows from the vast herds of the Dons south of the Border. Many a prominent business man, looked up to in the community began by evading the customs charges on goods crossing the Line.

No, he did not have anything to report concerning Ringo and his associates, even had he desired to do so. Better to just forget the whole business.

He was, in fact, rather glad to so do. He couldn't help but like John Ringo, a man splendidly brave, doubtless utterly upright in his relations with those he chose to call his friends, whose word, once given, was inviolable. Carson had a genuine feeling of regret that such a man should have made such a tragic ruin of a life that might have accomplished much and reached great heights instead of descending to a career of tragic futilities.

The dusk was sifting down from the flanks of the Dragoons like blue powder as Carson rode into town. Across the mesquite mesa, Tombstone was a nebulous shadow beneath its smoke pall. To the south, the crests of the Huachucas were ringed about with saffron flame. The last fiery rays of the setting sun flung zenithward from behind the distant Whetstones in the west. The wide rangeland was a purple and amethyst mystery, with only the yipping howl of a moon-waiting coyote or the lonely plaint of an owl perched high on a blasted pine to break the brooding silence. The scene was beautiful, but sad; sad, perhaps, with an excess of beauty, and despite the far-flung loveliness, Carson felt a sense of oppression as the night closed down and the silver loneliness of the stars spangled the blue-black sky.

After a thorough clean-up and a good night's sleep, Carson repaired to the general store and made some much needed purchases, paying for them with the hundred-dollar bill he had received from Hill. Then he settled down once more to the business of waiting for patients.

Two days later he had a visitor—three of them in fact. The bustling little man who first mounted the steps to his office he recognized as Johnny Behan, Sheriff of Cochise county. Behind him came handsome, smiling Billy Breakenridge and Jack Young, two of Behan's deputies.

The sheriff entered the office, took the chair Carson offered him, and immediately got down to business.

" Carson," he said, " the other day yuh changed a hundred dollar bill at the store here in Poce, didn't yuh? "

" Reckon that's right," Carson admitted. " Why? "

Behan ignored the question.

" Where'd yuh get that bill, Carson? " he shot at the young doctor.

Carson's eyes hardened a trifle at the sheriff's peremptory tone.

"What difference does that make?" he asked quietly.

"It makes plenty," Behan answered grimly. "That bill was part of the haul taken from the Poce Bank."

Carson stared at the sheriff.

"How do you know that?" he demanded.

"The bank keeps a record of the serial numbers of big bills," Behan replied. "There were only a few hundreds lifted in that robbery. We've been on the lookout for them. How'd yuh come to have that bill in yore possession?"

Tom Carson looked at the sheriff without seeing him. His mouth was suddenly dry as a light broke upon him.

Hill's vengeance for his bullet smashed hand—the vengeance of a crafty, vindictive man, a bully and a coward, but with the viciousness of a broken-back rattler.

"And I fell for it!" Carson muttered to himself. "If I hadn't been so up against it for some dinero, mebbe I'd have thought a little before accepting that bill. I'd ought to have known Hill had it in for me—he showed it more than once during the week—and known there was something funny about his being so all-fired generous all of a sudden! Well—"

In a few terse sentences he explained to Behan the circumstances under which he had come into possession of the bill. The sheriff looked deeply incredulous. There was a calculating gleam in his eye as it rested on Carson.

"It's a funny yarn," he commented, "some folks would say too damn funny."

Tom Carson didn't have any trouble following the sheriff's mental processes. Johnny Behan was a politician, and no amateur at the game. He was canny and sly and crafty, and he never missed a bet to further his interests in the deep and subtle game of politics. His administration was repeatedly and severely criticized, particularly because of his complacent relations with the outlaws of the deserts and mountains that ringed Tombstone. He strove to offset this criticism by sudden and spectacular coups which would rivet public attention on him and show him up in a favourable light. Carson realized that in this particular instance, Johnny Behan saw opportunity. He was not in the least surprised when the sheriff said—

" Reckon yuh'd better take a little ride to Tombstone with us, Carson, and tell yore story to Judge Wallace."

Tom Carson spent the night in the Tombstone jail. The hearing was set for two o'clock the following afternoon. The courtroom was crowded to the doors with onlookers when the bailiffs rapped for order.

As he was led in, Carson bitterly resented the curious stares directed at him, and the buzz of comment. He stood stiffly erect, his lean jaw set tight, his eyes the colour of frosted steel under a grey sky.

The Poce storekeeper testified that Carson had tendered the bill in payment for articles purchased at the store. A Poce Bank official identified the bill, by its serial number, as part of the loot taken from the bank in the course of the robbery. Sheriff Behan told that he had learned that Carson had been practically without funds for some time.

Carson took the stand and retold the story of how he had come into possession of the hundred-dollar bill. The judge listened intently, his grizzled brows drawing together. The crowd breathlessly awaited his verdict. The judge bent his stern gaze upon Carson's face.

" Mr. Defendant," he said, " the story you have told the court verges on the fantastic. I feel that you come close to sheer impudence in offering it to the court. It appears unbelievable to me that you should, as you say you did, accept money under such circumstances and from such an individual as you picture the man Hill without assuring yourself of his right to proffer it. Of course, admitting the possible truth of your explanation, you could justify yourself on the grounds of services rendered and maintain that, not being an officer of the law, you could not be expected to investigate the antecedents of the fee you received. That much the court is forced to admit. But even so, such an explanation predicates a woeful disregard of the ethics of an honourable profession. And why you should, as you said, refuse money from one man, who, in your expressed opinion, doubtless acquired said money in a questionable mean, and then turn around and accept money from another, who according to your story, offered some cock-and-bull explanation as to how it lawfully came into his possession, is beyond the understanding of the court. However—" he paused, studied Carson's whitening face an instant, then turned his gaze to Johnny Behan.

"However, Mr. Sheriff," he repeated, "unless you can offer further evidence that will tend to show active participation on the part of this defendant in the robbery to the Poce Bank the court will be forced to discharge said defendant. Inconsistent though his explanation of his possession of the note in question may sound, still you have offered no evidence to contradict it. Too often, of late, the court has bound over to the Grand Jury defendants you have brought into court on dubious evidence. The Grand Jury has consistently refused to indict. This puts the court in a bad light. The court feels that the mere possession of the stolen note by the defendant would not influence the Grand Jury sufficiently to justify bringing in a true bill. And if the Grand Jury did indict, the court feels that a trial jury would refuse to convict. The sheriff will recall that last year a defendant was hailed into this court on flimsy evidence. The Grand Jury brought in a true bill, nevertheless, and the defendant went to trial, and was adjudged innocent by the trial jury. Later, indubitable evidence of the defendant's guilt came to light; but under his constitutional rights, he could not be put in jeopardy a second time for the same offence. Result, a guilty man went free because of faulty court procedure. I do not care for a repetition of such an incident. I repeat, unless you can offer further evidence in support of your charge, I will be forced to discharge the defendant."

Sheriff Behan stood up. "Yore honour," he said, "I have done my duty as I saw it. The defendant admitted possession of the stolen note. I felt that the fact warranted an investigation in open court. It is not my place to judge the guilt or innocence of an accused. That is for the honourable Court to do. I bow to the Court's ruling; I have no further evidence to offer."

Carson's lips tightened. Johnny Behan had put it over—had showed himself in the light of a zealous peace officer doing his duty as he saw it. Carson himself was not cleared of the charge brought against him. It was just a case of not proven. Behan had gone up a notch in the estimation of the community; Carson was under a cloud. If his innocence was ever to be conclusively proven, it was up to him, Carson, to bring forth the evidence. The sheriff had washed his hands of the affair.

Tom Carson did not suffer any illusion concerning his present status. The remarks of Judge Wallace had been damning. The judge had plainly intimated that he did not believe Carson's story, although unable to refute it, and had, to all purposes, admitted that he was withholding action in the hope that further evidence might be uncovered that would substantiate Sheriff Behan's charge and prove Carson's complicity in the Poce Bank robbery. Undoubtedly, many people would consider him guilty of participation in the robbery and just naturally too damn smart to be pinned down. In the eyes of the community, he wore the owlhoot brand, and he would continue to wear it until his admittedly rather fantastic story was corroborated. His only hope was to run down Jim Hill and, in some way or other, force him to come forward with the admission that would clear Carson. Hill was the only man living who could back up his story. And forcing Hill to back up was liable to be some chore!

He knew he could not look to any of the owlhoot band to substantiate it. For them to do so would mean shoving their own necks into a noose.

Carson's face was bleak as he walked out of the clearing courtroom. There was a hot glow in the back of his grey eyes as his thoughts dwelt with the bearded outlaw.

Still thinking furiously, Carson walked along Allen Street.

At the corner of Fifth, he turned into the Oriental saloon. He felt badly in need of a drink.

Curious glances were darted in his direction as he walked along the bar to the far end, but nobody spoke to him. He found a vacant place near the end of the bar. Just beyond him stood two men, who eyed him silently as he breasted the bar.

The one nearest Carson was tall and blond and perhaps a little over thirty years old, although he looked considerably older. His face was long, with a peculiar pallor; his deepset eyes were blue-grey. He had a powerful looking chin; his hardset mouth was shaded by a tawny moustache that drooped beneath the edges of his jaws. There was something lion-like in his yellow mane of hair and in the slow but certain movements of his gaunt, heavily-boned, loose-limbed and powerful frame. Carson recognized Wyatt Earp, the " Lion of Tombstone," United States deputy-marshal, part owner of the Oriental, and candidate for sheriff of Cochise county.

Standing just beyond Wyatt Earp was a tall, extremely slender, ash-blond, grey-eyed man immaculately attired in grey. There was a look of refinement about his emaciated and very white face, but there was a light in the depths of his fine eyes that was disquieting. This was Doc Holliday, the fighting ace of the Earp faction, the deadliest and coldest-blooded killer in Tombstone.

Wyatt Earp took a step toward Carson. He spoke, a booming, lion-brool note in his deep voice.

" Son," he invited, " have a drink with me and Doc. I was in the co'ht room while you were on trial."

Tom Carson let his level grey gaze rest on Wyatt Earp's face, which had the cold stillness of sculptured stone.

" Yes? " he said quietly.

" Yes," Wyatt Earp repeated, " and I just want to tell yuh that I believe yore yarn. Yuh may be a lot of things, but I don't figger a liar is one of them."

" That's right," nodded the cheerful Holliday as he waved to the barkeeper to fill the glasses.

Tom Carson felt a sudden warm glow envelop him. Wyatt Earp was a power in Tombstone, and he enjoyed a reputation for calm unafraidness, for loyalty, devotion to duty and steadfastness that few men could boast.

" That—that's mighty fine of yuh, Mr. Earp," Carson said.

Wyatt Earp nodded slowly. " Yeah, we believe yuh were tellin' the truth," he said; " but there's one point I want to make. John Ringo is my enemy—he's sworn to kill me and Doc and my brothers, and he'll do it if he gets the chance—but nobody could make me believe that Ringo was a party to any such lowdown trick as was pulled on you. Ringo is pizen, but he's a square shooter and he could no more break his given word than he could sprout wings."

" I had something the same feeling," Carson admitted.

Wyatt Earp regarded his glass with a speculative eye.

" The jigger yuh ran up against is Jim Hill," he remarked. " Hill ain't his real name. He's the black sheep member of one of the best families in Arizona. He's mean as a striped snake and ornery enough to eat off the same plate. It's just the kind of a trick yuh could figger on Hill pullin'. He's plumb venomous. Look out for him, son."

" Yes," Carson replied grimly, " I'll certainly look out for him! "

Wyatt Earp studied the bleak face a moment, and nodded to himself.

" Son," he said abruptly, " I'd take it as a favour if yuh'd drop in and see me again in the next few days."

Carson glanced at him questioningly, but Wyatt did not see fit to amplify the request.

" Okay," Carson agreed. " I've got a little chore to look after right now, but I'll be in before long."

Wyatt Earp gave him a quick look, a look that seemed to evince understanding. Doc Holliday nodded as if Carson had explained something with elaborate detail. Carson shook hands with Earp and Holliday and left the saloon. Several men nodded in an agreeable fashion, as he passed along the bar, and more than one said " Howdy, Doc? "

Carson realized that the friendly overtures of Wyatt Earp and Doc Holliday were not devoid of value.

Wyatt Earp's gaze followed his tall figure out of the door.

" Yuh know, Doc," he said to his companion," that young feller reminds me of somebody—somebody I used to know up in Abilene, Kansas, or Dodge City—especially his eyes."

" I felt that way, too," Holliday agreed.

Earp tugged at his tawny moustache, and ruminated. Suddenly his eyes brightened.

" Doc!" he exclaimed, " I've got it. He reminds me of Bill Hickok!"

" By gosh! Wyatt, yuh've hit it!" Holliday agreed. " He has got the same kind of eyes as Wild Bill. Only he ain't as good looking as Wild Bill."

" That's right," admitted Wyatt Earp. " Wild Bill Hickok was so good looking it hurt; but this young feller has got a steadiness about him that Wild Bill didn't have. Wild Bill was just a fighter with a true eye and a fast gun hand. This feller has got all that too, or I'm a heap mistaken; but there's more to him than that. He's got a head on his shoulders that he uses for somethin' else 'sides holdin' up his hat. Doc, he's the kind of feller I'd like to have standin' at my back when the goin' was tough. I wouldn't have to worry about what went on behind me."

Which, coming as it did from the famous Marshal of Ellsworth and Dodge, packed considerable weight.

After leaving the Oriental, Carson obtained his horse and headed for Poce. A silent crowd was gathered on the porch of the general store as he rode past. Nobody spoke to him, but curious glances were cast in his direction. He could sense the subdued buzz of conjecture behind him. He stabled his horse, cooked and ate a frugal meal in his living quarters, and went to bed.

But not to sleep for many hours. His brain was a jumble of thoughts, speculations, half formed plans. Finally he did sleep, the sleep of mental exhaustion but he was awake before the dawn cast its red mantle over the lonely mountains.

The east was primrose and gold and the mighty shoulders of the Dragoons were still swathed in dusky purple as he buckled on his guns, saddled his horse and turned its head eastward.

Full day was just breaking when Carson entered the shadowy canyon that slashed the foothills. He rode for several miles, then turned from the trail and forced his horse through a tangle of thicket toward where he could hear a ripple of running water. In a small clearing beside a tiny trickle of stream he left the cayuse to graze. Then with infinite caution he continued his way on foot.

" If I go clattering up there on horseback, anybody within a mile will hear me coming and be on the lookout for me," he told himself as he stealthily advanced from one clump of brush or stone to another, stopping from time to time to peer and listen.

He reached the crevice in the canyon wall, paused to listen intently. No sound came from its dark depths. He stepped toward it, hands close to his guns; but this time no rifle bearing figure materialized from the cliff face. He cautiously entered the cleft and stole along its winding course. Far overhead the blue thread of sky lay on the black crests of the precipices. The shadows were thick at the bottom. His breathing sent soft, sighing echoes crawling up the splintered walls of stone.

Finally he reached the inner mouth of the cleft. He paused, standing well back in the shadows, and peered forth. Nobody was in sight. Then abruptly he heard a sound—the impatient stamp of a tethered horse.

Carson watched and listened for several minutes. No further sound broke the silence; there was no sign of movement on the little plateau outside the cleft mouth. He stepped forth boldly, glided toward the cave mouth, paused again to listen. Then he took another step forward.

" Come on in, Doc," a voice said from the darkness.

Chapter 3

TOM CARSON'S hands streaked to his guns. They froze gripping the black butts when he saw, by the half-light inside the cave, John Ringo leaning against the rock wall, calmly smoking a cigarette.

" Thought you'd be dropping along soon," observed Ringo, adding:

" But like me, you got here too late."

" What do you mean? " Carson asked.

" I mean there's nobody here but me," Ringo replied, taking a deep drag at his cigarette. He carefully pinched out the butt and dropped it to the ground.

" I was in the back of the court room during your hearing," he said. " As soon as Wallace turned you loose, I slipped out and hightailed here. But when I arrived, there was nobody here."

" Why did yuh ride here? " Carson asked curiously.

" To kill Jim Hill," was Ringo's simple reply.

" To kill Hill! "

" That's right. When he doublecrossed you, Doc, he also doublecrossed me, and a man who doublecrosses me doesn't live over long, if I'm able to line sights with him."

There was a cold, deadly finality to the statement that gave Carson a shivery feeling along his spine.

" I got word night before last you were in trouble," Ringo went on. " Finn Clanton rode here and said the sheriff had locked you up in Tombstone. Finn didn't know what it was all about, but figured I'd better know. I thought perhaps it had something to do with you coming here to treat Billy Clanton's wound, so I headed straight for Tombstone. I heard you tell your story and knew Jim Hill had put one over on you—and on me, too. Hill is mean as an Apache.

He didn't forget what you did to him when he tried to blindfold you, and figured to get even."

Ringo paused, drew himself to his full height and looked Carson squarely in the eye.

" Doc," he said, " I want to tell you that neither I, nor any of the other boys, to the best of my knowledge, had anything to do with that bank robbery."

" I believe yuh, if yuh say so," Carson returned quietly.

" Thanks," Ringo nodded. " It is evident that Hill did have. I could account for the movements of most of the boys the day the bank was robbed. All but Hill and Frank Stillwell and Pete Spence. I don't say that Stillwell or Spence had anything to do with it, but Hill evidently did have. Otherwise, how could he have gotten hold of that bill and know it came from the bank? "

" I've got to find Hill," Carson said.

John Ringo looked at the young man, and there was a strange expression in his sombre eyes.

" Doc," he said, " I've a notion it would be best if you forgot all about Hill. I know how you feel—and I also know what comes of that feeling. When I was about your age, I became involved in a war between cattle and sheep men. My only brother was killed in the feud—shot down in cold blood. I tracked down his three murderers and killed them all. Then I had to take it on the run to escape the law. I've been on the run ever since. Doc, the red road of vengeance often has a mighty black ending. Looking back now, I tell you it isn't worth it. You're young—you've got your life before you. If you keep your head straight on your shoulders, I predict the time will come when men will speak of you with respect and admiration, and, what's more, you'll be able to do an almighty lot of good. It isn't right to throw all that away just to gratify a thirst for revenge."

Tom Carson stared at the tall outlaw. Here was a side to John Ringo not generally known.

" I understand what yuh mean, Ringo," he made reply. " But it's not altogether revenge that's sending me after Hill.

Plenty of folks believe and will keep on believing, that I was mixed up in that bank robbery. Hill is the only man who can clear me."

"I can come forward and back up your story," Ringo suggested. "I figured on doing it there in court, if Wallace hadn't turned you loose. And folks know I don't lie."

"But you couldn't clear me," Carson pointed out. "You didn't see Hill give me that hundred-dollar note. You didn't even know he gave it to me until the story came out in court. Sure yuh could say I came here to treat Billy Clanton. Who brought me here? Hill! Why did Hill pick *me* to come out and treat Clanton? Why didn't he go to Tombstone and get a doctor of experience and repute to treat a man dangerously wounded? It's not a secret that there are doctors in Tombstone, and elsewhere, who are on sorta friendly terms with you and Bill Graham and others of yore outfit. It would seem logical that Hill would have picked one of them. Folks will say he picked me because he wanted a man he could trust, who was on friendly terms with him. Wouldn't you say that if yuh didn't know different?"

"Guess that's so," Ringo was forced to admit. "The fact that Hill picked you because he knew Billy needed a doctor as quickly as he could get one wouldn't count. He saw your shingle as he was riding through Poce on the way to Tombstone and decided to take a chance on you. Yes, you've reasoned the thing out right, Doc."

For some minutes the tall outlaw was silent, his eyes brooding.

"Hill will be on the run," he said, almost as if talking to himself. "He knew the jig was up when Finn Clanton rode in with the word that Johnny Behan had picked you up. Yes, he'll be on the run from now on—from you and from me: but I've a notion I know where to find him, for a little while, anyhow. Come on, Doc, you and me are going to take a ride."

Ringo obtained his horse where it was tethered in a thicket not far from the cave mouth. Then they passed through the cleft and retrieved Carson's mount. Ringo led the way across the Dragoons, following a trail Carson had never heard of and which, he shrewdly surmised, was known to the outlaws alone. Finally the shimmering, sunny reaches of Sulphur Springs Valley lay below them. Far across the valley were the blue crests of the Chiricahuas. At their feet was the road that· led to Galeyville, the capital of Curly Bill Graham's outlaw kingdom.

" Hill won't go to Galeyville," Ringo observed, " but I've a notion I know where he will hang out for a little while. Hill is a queer jigger. I understand he has Indian blood. Anyhow, he's got friends among a bunch of ornery halfbreeds and Yaquis who hang out in the Chiricahuas and down below the Line. The chances are he aims to hole up with them for a spell or drift down into Sonora. If he figures on that, he's almost sure to meet with them where we are going, and tonight should be the night."

They descended to the valley and rode along the Galeyville road. It was full dark when they reached what Ringo said was Myers Cinega. Here Ringo turned aside and they rode for some distance up a wide gulch until a light showed through the trees.

" This is Patterson's boozing ken," Ringo said in low tones. " Here's where we will find Jim Hill, if my hunch is correct. We'll leave our horses here among the trees. Take it easy, and be ready for trouble. There may be a fight."

Carson loosened his guns in their holsters and he and Ringo stole softly towards the light. Soon a gaunt building loomed amid the trees.

With catlike tread, Ringo led the way to the closed front door. Inside was the sound of loud voices raised in drunken wrangling.

" Okay," said Ringo, and flung open the door.

Carson was dazzled for an instant by the light within. Then he saw a low-ceiled room with a bar running across the far end. By the light of a single hanging lamp he observed a number of dark-faced men at the bar, who turned at the sound of the opening door.

As he and Ringo stepped into the room, there was a warning

hiss. Carson had a fleeting glimpse of a tall bearded man with glittering black eyes at the far end of the bar. He recognized Jim Hill before the latter dodged behind his companions, his hands streaking down.

Carson whipped his own guns from their sheaths; but even as he cleared leather, there was the roar of a shot, a terrific clang-jangling of rending metal and shattered glass. The big hanging lamp seemed to fly to pieces. Darkness swooped down and blanketed the room.

Carson went sideways along the wall, conscious that Ringo was beside him. Lances of fire spurted from the darkness. Bullets drummed against the wall. The room seemed to rock and sway to the rear of sixshooters.

Weaving and ducking, Carson fired at the flashes with both hands. He heard a yell, a queer coughing grunt, then a terrific crash, a splintering of wood and the tinkle of falling glass. Beside him he could see the blaze of Ringo's gun and hear the thunder-roll of the reports. He leaped across the room, tripped over something and measured his length on the floor.

Despite the jar of his fall, Carson retained his guns. He rolled over on his side, fired at a shadow figure, and rolled again. Somewhere a door banged open. He heard Ringo curse venomously in low tones, and the thud of his boots crossing the room. He leaned to his feet and groped after his companion. An instant later he butted into Ringo, who was twisting a door knob and swearing.

" The hellions locked the door after them," Ringo growled. " Hold it a minute and listen. I thought so! Horses! Listen to those irons clatter! "

Carson could hear the beat of hoofs fading into the distance. Ringo struck a match and by the flicker of its flame they surveyed the room.

Two men lay on the floor, without sound or motion. From behind the bar rose a white face.

" Don't shoot! It's me—Patterson! " called the face. " Wait a minute—I'll get a lamp."

C

A light glowed back of the bar.   Patterson placed the lighted lamp on the " mahogany " and wiped his ashen face with a bar towel.

" What in blazes is the matter, John? " he demanded. " What was all the shootin' about? "

" How long has Jim Hill been here? " Ringo asked, ignoring the questions.

" About two hours.   He rode up and asked if I had seen you or Curly Bill.   Said he was headin' for Galeyville but figgered on meetin' some friends here fust.   An hour later them breeds and Yaquis came along.   I gathered that Hill was goin' somewhere with 'em.   They were just about ready to leave when you fellers blowed in.   What's it all about? I thought Hill was a friend of yores? "

Again Ringo did not choose to answer the barkeep's question. He stared sombrely at the smashed window by way of which Jim Hill had taken his departure, his brows black and frowning.

Carson was looking over the two dead men.   They had swarthy faces with high cheek bones and thin lips.   Their glazing eyes were beadily black.

" Yaquis breeds, I'd say," he muttered.   " Salty looking jiggers."

" Have your swampers carry them out and dump them in a hole, and then forget about what happened here tonight," Ringo told the barkeeper.   "You can put us up for the night. First I want a few drinks.   I hope I winged Jim Hill so he'll die somewhere out in the brush with the buzzards picking his eyes out and the ants gnawing his ears."

Carson and Ringo were on the move early next morning.

" I don't think there's much chance that Hill rode to Galeyville," the latter observed, " but we'll go and see. Perhaps somebody there may give us a line on him."

They rode on across Sulphur Springs Valley and followed the road where it wound its way across the Chiricahuas and descended the eastern slopes.   They passed Silver Creek Canyon and came to a point where the mountains opened out into an amphitheatre.   They climbed to a stony mesa.

Through the mouth of the canyon a few miles away, they could catch a glimpse of the San Simon Valley. To the west towered the main range of the Chiricahuas, a misty blue wall shouldering the bluer blue of the sky.

The main street of Galeyville ran along the edge of the mesa. On one side stood a row of saloons and stores facing Turkey Creek bottoms. On the opposite side of the street was a single saloon boasting the name, " Nick Babcock's."

Sitting in the chair under a live oak in front of the saloon was a round-faced, black-eyed jovial looking man with a shock of curly black hair. He was heavy-set, almost rotund looking, but his moves were panther like. In one hand he held a bottle of beer from which he took an occasional swig. In the other he held a six shooter.

As Ringo and Carson rode up, the beer bottle tilted over the curly headed man's head, the neck to his lips. At the same instant his gun flipped outward. Smoke wisped from the muzzle. A tin can perhaps a hundred feet distant leaped spasmodically into the air.

" Howdy, Curly?" called Ringo. " I see you happened to hit one for a change,"

" Hello, John," replied the other. " Who's yore friend? "

" This is Doc Carson, Curly, who kept Billy Clanton from taking the big jump," Ringo replied. " Doc, know Bill Graham—a friend of mine."

" Howdy, Doc," acknowledged Curly Bill. " Light off and have a drink."

" We're looking for Jim Hill," Ringo vouchsafed as they dismounted.

Curly Bill evinced no surprise. " Figgered yuh would be," he admitted. " I heard about what happened in Tombstone. Hill ain't been here, and I don't figger he will be."

As they entered the saloon, Ringo acquainted Graham with what had happened the night before at Patterson's roadhouse. The outlaw chieftain nodded gravely.

" John," he said a little later, " yuh know, I've had a notion for some time that Hill was goin' to pull out and start on his own. That's why he's been gangin' with them Yaquis and breeds. I've a feelin' that he's goin' to give Johnny Behan somethin' real to worry about. Hill ain't got no use for Johnny, and he's liable to make it hot for that fat sheriff."

" And make it easier for Wyatt Earp to win the shrievalty contest," Ringo commented grimly.

Curly Bill looked grave. " It wouldn't be good for us fellers for Wyatt Earp to get elected sheriff," he conceded. " We can do business with Johnny Behan, but Earp hates our guts. So long as he's just a dep'ty United States Marshal and sticks inside of Tombstone, he ain't nothin' for us to worry about: but sheriff of Cochise county! Gentlemen, hush! John, that damn Hill is liable to become a plumb nuisance."

" What's what I figure," agreed Ringo. " I've a notion we're going to hear from Hill mighty soon, and in a way we won't like."

Chapter 4

IT was mid afternoon when the Benson stage pulled out of Tombstone. Bud Philpot was on the driver's seat. Bob Paul the shotgun messenger, shared the seat with the driver. There were six passengers inside the coach, and three on top. In the boot, in an innocent looking wooden box was eighty thousand dollars. The big shipment was a dead secret, or supposed to be.

The big, lumbering coach jogged along easily, Philpot was saving his horses for the hard pull through the hills. Philpot and Paul chatted amicably as the stage rumbled over the ruts in the road, stirring up a little cloud of dust that danced like golden smoke in the mellow sunshine. The passengers drowsed in their seats, all unsuspecting that grim tragedy was waiting farther along the road.

They reached Contention, ten miles from Tombstone. There Paul took the driver's place, so Philpot could rest his hands and stretch his legs. He leaned his shotgun between his legs. Philpot lounged easily, half drowsing with the passengers.

Six miles farther on they crossed a wide and deep dry wash and began climbing a sharp grade. The horses strained at the traces, the stage creaked and groaned on its springs. A walk was the best speed the horses could make with the heavy vehicle.

The afternoon was well along now. The sun was flaming downward toward the crests of the Huachucas, whose flanks and shoulders were already swathed with purple shadows. There was an early evening chill in the air. Slowly and still more slowly crawled the stage, lurching between thick growths of mesquite that flanked the trail on either side.

Suddenly there was a crackling in the brush. Three masked

men bulged from the growth with levelled rifles. A voice rang out—

"Hold it!"

Philpot's head jerked up. A passenger cried out with alarm. Bob Paul dropped the reins and grabbed his shotgun. The highwayman on his side of the road pulled trigger. A bullet thudded into the seat scant inches from Paul's body. Without raising the shotgun to his shoulders he fired both barrels.

Echoing the double roar boomed a shot from the far side of the road. Philpot straightened on the seat, whirled sideways and plunged downward. His falling body struck the heels of the wheelers. With frightened squeals the horses lunged ahead. The reins went whipping to the ground. . . .

At a mad run the frantic horses tore up the grade, the stage lurching and careening. Behind sounded a drumroll of gunfire. An outside passenger, Peter Roerig of Tombstone, gave a choking cry, leaped to his feet as if galvanized and pitched headlong to the ground. Bullets thudded into the rear of the coach as it careened wildly over the crest of the sag.

The maddened horses swerved. They left the road and went tearing through the brush. The wheels banged against rocks, dipped into holes. The clumsy coach lurched and swayed, sometimes with two wheels in the air. The terrified passengers clung to their seats and shrieked their fear.

Bob Paul dropped his shotgun, gripped the dashboard with both hands and lowered himself until his feet were on the tongue. Swaying, reeling, risking his life twice a second, he strained down and groped until his fingers clutched the reins. Clinging with one hand, he drew them up. Then, with a mighty effort, he regained the driver's seat. He tightened his grip on the reins and put forth all his strength. But the maddened horses took no heed. On they tore, regardless of obstacles. Paul fought them with every trick known to the teamster. Fully a mile passed, with death striking viciously every foot of the way, before he got the team under control. He headed the stage back to the highway. At a lathering gallop he brought the stage into Benson. The coach was riddled with bullets, the passengers near collapse from fear and suspense, but the eighty thousand dollars in the boot was safe.

Sheriff Behan and his posse took the trail the following morning as soon as it was light. Included among the possemen were Wyatt, Virgil and Morgan Earp. They picked up the owlhoots' trail, which led east to the Dragoons. Grimly they followed it, threading their way through the canyons and over the crests.

Carson and John Ringo left Galeyville the afternoon of the second day following the Benson Road holdup. Ringo and Curly Bill and others had indulged in a prolonged drinking bout. But aside from a slight redness around his sombre eyes, Ringo showed no signs of his potations.

Beyond where Morse's Canyon opens out into Sulphur Springs Valley, on a steep bank that rose from some distance west of and below Coyote Smith's ranchhouse, which stood in open timber, they paused for a short while in the shade of a giant live oak of peculiar formation; it consisted of five thick trunks rising from a stump-like central stem. Here in days to come, John Ringo was to die under mysterious circumstances, never fully made clear. They smoked a cigarette before riding on. Ringo glanced gloomily about, perhaps chilled by a vague premonition, for it seemed to Carson that he shuddered slightly as his gaze rested on a flat rock held in position by the five trunks and forming a seat in the cool shade. Then, with a shrug of his broad shoulders, he rode on, Carson stirrup to stirrup with him.

As they approached the foothills of the Dragoons, they saw a dust cloud bearing toward them along the trail.

" Somebody fogging it for fair," remarked Ringo as he studied the cloud with narrowed lids.

Soon the cloud resolved into a number of horsemen approaching at a great rate. A few minutes more and they were able to recognize Sheriff Johnny Behan at the head of the group. Riding stirrup to stirrup behind him were Wyatt and Virgil Earp.

The posse pulled their horses to a walk as they drew near. Sheriff Behan stared at Ringo and Carson, and brought his mount to a halt. He addressed himself to Tom Carson in sarcastic tones.

"Another one of yore friends get gunned up back in the hills—by accident?" he asked.

"Not—yet!" Carson replied quietly, spacing his words.

The sheriff glared at him. Wyatt Earp nodded cordially. He and Virgil Earp, a stern looking, taciturn man of soldierly bearing, glowered at Ringo, and Ringo glowered back. Morgan Earp, youthful, yellow-haired, straight and stalwart, with a strong young fighter's face, also frowned heavily, his bold blue-grey eyes resting hotly on the saturnine Ringo.

"What's up, Johnny—going for a ride?" asked Ringo.

"Did yuh see two hellions hightailin' it along this way?" Sheriff Behan asked a question of his own.

"Nope," replied Ringo. "We rode from Galeyville and didn't meet anybody on the road. What's up?"

In sulphurous language, Sheriff Behan regaled them with an account of the holdup.

"We got a feller we figger to be one of 'em," he concluded. "He was loaded down with guns and ammunition and was milkin' a cow up on Redfield's ranch. He's a cowboy named Luther King, and used to work for Redfield. He admitted a tuckered out horse we picked up at Wheaton's abandoned ranch belonged to him, but he wouldn't admit anythin' else, so far. We got him corralled in the Tombstone jail. The other two keep givin' us the dodge."

All the while he was speaking, the sheriff's narrowed glance rested on Tom Carson's face. He seemed to hesitate before riding on.

"Let's get goin', Johnny," urged Wyatt Earp. "We're wastin' time."

"I'm not so sure that we are," countered the sheriff. He still hesitated, but Wyatt Earp pushed his horse ahead.

"I want to see yuh when I get back," he told Carson. "As soon as yuh reach town, drop into the Oriental and see Doc

Holliday. I left a message with him for you. I'll consider it a prime favour to me if yuh'll do what he says. Okay?"

"Okay," Carson promised wonderingly.

With a last glowering look, Sheriff Behan touched up his own horse. In a few minutes the posse was but a dust cloud in the distance.

John Ringo stared ruefully after the possemen.

"This helps you a lot," he told Carson. "Right this minute Johnny Behan is figuring we are the jiggers he's after. If you'd been with anybody else but me, I reckon he'd have dropped the loop on you."

"Could be," admitted Carson as they rode on.

Ringo rode for a long time in silence, then abruptly he spoke.

"Didn't I say we'd hear from Jim Hill mighty soon," he said.

"Yuh figger Hill was mixed up in that holdup?" asked Carson.

"I do," Ringo replied briefly. "That's where he and his Yaqui hellions were heading for from the Patterson roadhouse. But I'm willing to bet they never tie Jim Hill up with it. Nobody has ever been able to prove anything against Jim Hill. He's a cagey hombre. Handing you that hundred-dollar bill is the only time I ever knew him to slip up on anything. And that gives you a notion, Doc, what a hankering for revenge will do to a man. Makes him do things plumb against his better judgment and act as if his brains were addled. Keep away from it, Doc."

It was late when they reached Tombstone, but after stabling their horses, they immediately repaired to the Oriental. They found Doc Holliday there. To Carson's surprise, Holliday and Ringo greeted each other without the slightest show of unfriendliness. Carson was learning something about the laws of hospitality as observed by the Cochise county outlaws. Here Holliday was in the role of host, Ringo of a guest. There could be nothing but courteous intercourse between them so long as the status quo obtained.

"Carson," said Holliday. "There is a vacant room up at Wyatt Earp's place. He wants yuh to occupy it until he gets back to Tombstone. He said for yuh to eat here at the Oriental and drink all yuh want. Everything is on the House."

" But—" Carson started to protest.

" Wyatt asked yuh to do so as a personal favour to him," cut in Holliday. " I understand he has a business deal to talk over with yuh and asks that yuh stay here as his guest until he gets back—as a personal favour."

" Don't see how you can do anything else, Carson," interpolated Ringo. " You as much as promised Wyatt you would, out on the trail. Remember? "

" I reckon that's right," Carson accepted reluctantly.

Carson encountered John Ringo when he dropped into the Oriental the following morning for breakfast.

" Luther King has started talking," announced Ringo. " He says the three fellows who tried to rob the stage were Bill Leonard, Jim Crane and Harry Head. He swears he didn't know what they were up to. Says he was down in a hollow holding their horses while they went up the steep grade on foot to see a Mexican woodchopper about doing some work for them. The chopper was supposed to be cutting up above the Benson Trail. King says he didn't realize something was wrong until he heard the shooting up on the trail. It's a loco sounding yarn, but unless they drop a loop on those jiggers, there isn't much by which to prove that King is lying."

But soon afterward Tombstone began to seethe with rumours of still another man taking part in the attempted robbery, a man who was still walking the streets of Tombstone. Some said that Doc Holliday was the man. Others maintained that it was a man not generally known to be connected with the outlaw fraternity of Cochise county.

" So I'm a stage robber now, eh? " remarked the cheerful ex-dentist when apprised of what folks were saying. " Well! Well! I don't believe it! That eighty thousand got away, didn't it? That much dinero wouldn't get away from me if I was out to get it. Nope, I never will believe it! "

John Ringo had another notion.

" There was a fourth man, all right," he observed to Carson,

" and that fourth man wasn't Luther King, either. Carson, that fourth jigger, who stayed on the sidelines and directed things was Jim Hill. That's his way. And Hill was close friends with Leonard and Head and Crane. I believe Luther King is telling the truth."

Apparently others had something of the same notion, for shortly afterward Luther King escaped from custody under peculiar circumstances and was never heard of again.

" Yes, there was a fourth man, all right," said Sheriff Behan when he got back to town, " and I've a mighty good notion who that fourth man was, even though I can't prove it against him unless we catch one of the others and start him talkin'."

Tom Carson laboured under no illusions as to whom Johnny Behan referred when he spoke of the mysterious fourth man. Carson set his lips tight and said nothing.

Soon afterward, Tombstone learned that Leonard and Head had been killed at Owl City, New Mexico. Jim Crane also died, apparently at the hands of the Mexicans in Guadalupe Canyon.

" No witnesses against Jim Hill now," John Ringo observed grimly to Carson.

Carson " got " the implication, but refrained from uttering any superfluous comment.

In the meanwhile, Wyatt Earp had returned to town. He called Tom Carson into his private office, shut the door and motioned him to a chair. Occupying another chair was a dignified looking elderly man who nodded to Earp but did not speak. Earp addressed himself to Carson.

" One of the things I wanted to talk to yuh about is this," he said. " Two doors down from the Oriental is a vacant office. It's just the thing for a doctor. You hang yore shingle there and move to Tombstone; yuh'll starve to death in Poce, partickler since what happened. Reckon yuh've realized that by now."

" But there are already several good doctors in Tombstone," Carson objected.

" But not enough," Wyatt Earp countered. " The doctor

business is comin' in this pueblo. You do as I say. I've a notion yuh'll get patients."

Carson pondered a moment. "Okay," he agreed at last, "I'll do it."

Wyatt Earp nodded approval. "And now there's something else I want to talk to yuh about," he announced. He turned to the elderly man in the chair.

"Marshal," he said, "I want yuh to know Tom Carson. He's the young feller I was tellin' yuh about. Carson, this is Mr. C. P. Dade, United States Marshal of Arizona. He has somethin' to say to yuh."

Marshal Dade acknowledged the introduction with a nod.

"Want to make yuh an offer, Carson," he said. "Am offerin' yuh a job as a federal deputy marshal for the Tombstone district, assistant to Wyatt Earp. In fact, it was Wyatt's notion in the fust place."

"But—but—" stammered the astonished Carson.

"It's this way, Carson," Wyatt Earp broke in. "In the fust place, we all know yuh're tryin' yore best to run down Jim Hill. Well, that's all right, in a way. We know yuh want to get Hill inter co'ht and make him talk. That's okay, but the way yuh're goin' about it isn't okay. Yuh're takin' too big a chance of gettin' inter serious trouble yoreself. As a private citizen, yuh have no authority to molest Hill in any way. Remember, Jim Hill may be suspected of a lot of things, but he's never been convicted of any crime. The law has nothing on him. There is no real proof that he ever committed a crime, no matter what we think, any more than there is any proof that Frank Stillwell and Pete Spence ever held up a stage, although I'd be willin' to swear they did; but I couldn't prove a thing against them. S'pose yuh tangle with Hill, end up in a shootin' and cash him in? Yuh'd be up against a charge of murder, and don't think Johnny Behan wouldn't do everthin' in his power to press that charge and make it stick. Yuh'd be up against somethin' mighty bad, and yuh'd be lucky if yuh didn't end up in the penitentiary. Get the notion?"

Carson nodded. The way Wyatt Earp presented the case gave him something to think about.

" So here's what I figgered out," Earp continued: " Marshal Dade is just about sure for certain that Jim Hill had a hand in the robbery of the C. & P. passenger train a few months back. The robbers got gold that was part of an interstate shipment. That puts the affair within the jurisdiction of federal authorities. Marshal Dade is mighty anxious to drop a loop on Jim Hill. He figgers if he can get Hill inter custody, he can bring up enough evidence against Hill to get a confession outa him. Hill might talk to save his own skin, of that we're purty certain. But gettin' hold of Hill is provin' to be a considerable chore. Now if you hold a deputy marshal's commission, yuh have authority to act against Hill and take him inter custody. Yuh'll be a sorta undercover man—nobody will know yuh are a deputy marshal till the time comes for yuh to reveal the fact. I figger that, sooner or later, Hill will get tired of yuh trailin' him and try to come up for a showdown. He wouldn't do that if he knew yuh had peace officer connections. You will be accomplishin' yore own object, and furtherin' the ends of justice as well. Get the notion?"

" Yes," Carson agreed, " I think I do. I accept yore offer, and much obliged for it."

Wyatt Earp was right when he predicted Carson would get patients in Tombstone; but not even Wyatt Earp expected they would be what they were. Tom Carson very quickly found himself in a peculiar position.

Reputable citizens of Tombstone would have nothing of him. They made it plain that they would have been better pleased if Doctor Carson had hung his shingle elsewhere. Mayor Thomas visited his office and spoke to the point.

" We can do without yore kind in Tombstone, Carson," he said. " We got too many of that kind here already. I can't order yuh to get out, but if I have any influence here I'll see to it that yuh'll hafta get out—or starve."

But Tom Carson didn't " get out "; neither did he starve.

The friends and associates of John Ringo and Curly Bill Graham saw to that. Time after time Carson was called to some outlying ranch or cabin to treat men suffering from knife or gunshot wounds. They were uncommunicative as to how their injuries came about; but they were grateful for his ministering and paid in cash. Also, ranchers and claim workers who had no outlaw connections got into the habit of sending to town for Doctor Carson when in need of medical attention for themselves, their families or hands. These outlying spread owners, Carson knew, while not in league with the owlhoot faction of Cochise county, had a healthy respect for them and liked to be let alone by them. Carson shrewdly suspected that Ringo and Graham had quietly spread the word around that Doctor Carson was a good man to call when a physician was needed. Carson soon had what would be considered a snug practice for a young doctor. It was unconventional, perhaps, but it was remunerative.

Also, there was another angle that carried weight with Carson. In the course of his professional ministering, he was constantly thrown in contact with the kind of individuals who would be likely to have knowledge of Jim Hill and his whereabouts. Sooner or later, he figured, somebody would see fit to talk. A desire for revenge against Hill for some wrong, gratitude to Carson for his timely aid, a feeling that such action might help when the person vouchsafing the information would find himself at odds with the law—all these motives were to be considered. Carson knew this, and felt that he was on the right track.

John Ringo provided a partial explanation for this unconventional though remunerative practice that came to young Doctor Carson.

"The boys know about how you pulled Billy Clanton through," Ringo said. "They know, too, that you went and treated Billy after you'd hawgtied Jim Hill and didn't have to go unless you wanted to. They know, too, that you didn't say a word to anybody after you got back home, because you figured it wasn't a doctor's place to talk about his patients.

The boys have you down as a square-shooter, even though you are friendly with the Earps."

Yes, Tom Carson was " eating regularly," but he was not content. A feeling of injustice rankled in his heart. He bitterly resented the attitude of Tombstones' better citizens.

" Don't let it worry yuh overmuch, son," counselled kindly, experienced old Doctor Goodfellow, who from the beginning showed a fatherly interest in the young practitioner. " You just keep on doin' yore work right and they'll finally come around. I been gettin' reports on you from folks out in the hills. Out there they say yuh're a bang-up doctor. Don't let things get yuh down. Everythin' will work out in the end—it allus does. Just hang on to yore stirrups and don't pull leather. The Earps are yore friends, and the Earps are the right sort of folks, even though some people figger different. The fact is, it's the friendship of the Earps that is at the bottom of some of yore trouble. There's an almighty political row buildin' up hereabouts, with Johnny Behan and his outfit on the prod against the Earps, and Johnny is some pumpkins as a politician. But I've found that stickin' to the right sort of folks pays in the end. The time will come when these gents who turn up their noses at yuh will be comin' around to shake yore hand. Mark my word on it."

Carson also acquired another practice, which, while not particularly remunerative, proved to have an unexpected value. Many Mexicans worked in the mine, a large portion of them peons of the lowliest order. Carson learned that these poor people were not receiving their proper share of needed medical attention. Soon the tall young doctor was a familiar figure among the dobes and shacks where the labourers lived. Many a sick child regained health through his ministrations. Many a bread winner of a little family, incapacitated by injury, was again able to provide the simple needs of his loved ones because of the frequent visits and tireless attentions of El Curador—The Healer—as they called him.

And Tom Carson soon discovered that the heartfelt gratitude

of these humble people meant more than fat fees or even the approval of the older and more experienced doctors of Tombstone.

But most of the respectable citizens continued to look askance at Carson.   They shared Johnny Behan's disbelief of his explanation concerning his possession of the hundred dollar bill that had been part of the Poce Bank robbery loot. Others pointed out his friendship with John Ringo and Doc Holliday.

Holliday himself was under a cloud.   That he had taken part in the abortive holdup of the Benson stage was firmly believed by many, although no formal charges were ever brought against the ex-dentist.   Which, incidentally, bothered the cheerful desperado not at all.

But Tom Carson had different feelings about the suspicion directed toward him, and despite John Ringo's advice and warning, there grew within him a feeling of vindictive hatred of Jim Hill.   He knew that his only chance of clearing his name was to get Hill into court and force him to tell the truth concerning the incident.   All the efforts of his spare time were bent to this end.

Hill, however, proved most elusive.   So far as Carson's efforts to locate him were concerned, he might as well have dissolved into air.   If the Cochise county outlaws had any knowledge relative to his whereabouts, they kept it to themselves.

" He's a shrewd hombre," said John Ringo.   " He's cold and calculating and patient.   Most owlhooters sooner or later put a rope around their own necks, but not Jim Hill. Right now, like as not, he's working at some respectable job.   He's done that before, kept in the clear until things cooled down and folks forgot about him.   You wouldn't think it to look at him or hear him talk, but he's a man of education and more than average intelligence.   You've got your work cut out for you, Doc."

And then, most unexpectedly, Carson got a line on Jim Hill.   He had been treating the sick child of a peon and was heading back up town through the narrow streets of the Mexican quarter when a shadowy figure stepped from the darkness, face muffled in a serape and shaded by a low drawn hat brim.

" Señor Medico," said the figure, " I would speak with you."

" Okay, fire away," Carson replied.

" Señor, if you will go to Garcia's cantina, without delay, you will see there a man who can lead you to one you greatly desire to find."

" But have a care, señor," the informant added quickly as Carson was about to speak. " The one at Garcia's is a muy male hombre."

Before Carson could question him, the muffled man had faded back into the shadows.

Carson stood still and considered. He knew that the Mexican quarter was fully aware of his desire to catch Jim Hill. Doubtless the tip he had just been given was from someone he had befriended, but who did not care to have his identity known in connection with the matter.

Garcia's, he knew, was a little wine shop where peons congregated. It was situated where the granite lion paw on which Tombstone was built sent out stony claws into the mesquite. Perhaps some associate of Hill's was taking his pleasure there; but how was he to spot his man? His informant had been confident that Carson would know the person he sought.

" It's worth trying, anyhow," he muttered as he hurried to his quarters.

The man would lead him to Hill, the informant said. Which would infer that the owlhoot was doubtless not in Tombstone or its environs. He had also said that the one in question was a " very bad man," which would mean that he would not lead Carson to Hill of his own accord.

" Meant I'd have to trail him to some hangout or other," Carson quickly deduced.

Hurriedly he got the rig on his horse. Almost mechanically he placed in his saddlebags the little case of medicines and

D

surgical instruments he always carried with him. As an afterthought he stowed some provisions also, including coffee. Included, too, was a small frying pan and a little flat tin pail. He buckled on his guns, shoved his heavy Winchester in the saddle boot, mounted and rode eastward toward the edge of the town.

Garcia's cantina stood alone amid the mesquite, in the shadow of a large tree. As Carson approached, he could see a golden bar of light streaming through a side window. Some distance from the building he dismounted and proceeded on foot. As he drew near, he heard the impatient stamping of a horse tied not far from the door. He crept cautiously to the window and peered in.

There were a number of peons in the room, some standing at the bar, others drinking at the tables; but Carson almost instantly spotted his man.

He stood at the end of the bar farthest from the door, which he faced, although he conversed across the bar with Garcia, who seemed perturbed about something. He was tall and rangy and lance-straight. His eyes were bits of polished obsidian in a face that was swarthy almost to blackness. He had high cheek bones set wide apart, a thinlipped gash of a mouth and a highbridged nose. His lank black hair was cut in a bang across his low forehead. He had a wild beast look about him and he moved his hands as a cat does its paws.

" Mighty nigh a pure blood Yaqui," Carson muttered. "One of Hill's outfit, sure as shooting."

For perhaps half an hour the Yaqui drank, downing glass after glass of firey tequila, addressing an occasional remark to Garcia, who kept drifting back to the end of the bar, his fat face mirroring uneasiness and concern. Finally, with a shrug of his sinewy shoulders and a last guttural remark, the Yaqui placed his empty glass on the bar and glided rather than walked across the room to the door. There he paused for an instant, cast a significant glance at the worried cantina owner, opened the door and passed out.

Carson, crouching low in the shadow of the tree, saw him

walk stealthily to where the horse stamped in the mesquite. A moment later his head and shoulders loomed above the low growth, faintly illumed by the starlight, and he rode away along a narrow trail that curved westward around the hills.

Carson waited a few minutes, then mounted and rode after him. He rounded a bend and saw his quarry, a misty shadow, some hundreds of yards ahead. Keeping well in the gloom of the brush that flanked the trail, he followed. The thick dust muffled the beat of his horse's hoofs and he had little fear of the Yaqui discovering he was trailed. The sky was sown with stars but was moonless and the night was dark.

South to the Huachucas led the trail. The great clock of the sky wheeled westward and the night grew darker. Carson took a chance and closed the distance somewhat, but the lone rider proceeded steadily with never a backward glance. The first greying of the eastern sky found them well among the foothills of the range, threading their way through a gloomy, brush grown canyon.

And now Carson had to fall back. The grey in the east had turned to primrose, to scarlet shot with bars of gold. Even in the narrow canyon the light was strengthening. He fell further behind, until the quarry was out of sight. But as far as he could see, there was but a single trail through the canyon. On either side was thick growth and a jumble of boulders and chimney rocks. Soon the light was strong enough for him to make out objects distinctly, and as the whole vast arch of the sky flooded with gold as an over-filled cup with yellow wine, he could see the hoofprints of the horse he was following.

Then came a stony stretch and the tracks were no longer visible. And a mile or so farther on the trail forked.

Carson pulled up with a muttered curse of exasperation. The canyon had widened greatly and the quarry could just as easily have gone one way as the other. He rode for a little distance along the left fork, scanning the ground closely; but the hard soil afforded no sign of a recent passage. He hesitated a moment, then turned back to the fork, dismounted and went over the ground with the greatest care.

Nothing showed at the fork. He turned right and bending low, closely scrutinized every inch of the soil.

Suddenly he uttered a sharp exclamation. Before him lay a small round boulder. This was not remarkable as the trail was strewn with stones. But the upper side of this particular boulder was moist and lightly encrusted with particles of damp earth.

"Horse's iron kicked it loose from its bed," Carson muttered. He searched carefully and a moment later found the round indenture in the earth where the boulder had been dislodged.

"Right! this is the way he came," Carson exulted. He forked his horse once more and rode along the right-hand branch of the trail. Ten minutes later he found fresh hoof marks on a patch of soft ground.

The trail diagonalled across the canyon. A few miles farther on it entered a much narrower side canyon that ran in a southwesterly direction. Here he found more evidence of the quarry's passing. The signs were fresher, too, evidence that he was gaining on the rider. He slowed down, for the brush was thick and the trail, little more than a game track, was winding. Suddenly he pulled his big roan to a halt and sniffed sharply. There was a whiff of wood smoke tanging the clear air.

For some minutes Carson sat his horse and debated what course to pursue. He was undoubtedly close to the man he was following. Had he stopped to build a fire and cook a meal, or was the owlhoot hangout nearby? Finally he touched up the roan and rode slowly forward, eyes and ears intent.

The smell of smoke grew stronger. Carson halted again. Now he could hear a sound, somewhere to the left. It was the tinkle of running water.

"The brush had oughta be thin along that crik bank over there," he told himself, "and I've a notion it runs parallel to this trail. I'll take a chance."

He turned the bay from the trail and pushed through the growth until he reached the bank of the little stream, which was about two hundred yards distant. As he expected, the bank was comparatively free from growth. He threaded his way among the scattered bushes, peering and listening. Again he reined in. Directly opposite him was a faint smudge rising against the blue of the sky. Where he had paused was a little grass grown clearing.

" You take it easy, feller, and fill yore belly," he told the horse as he dismounted. " And keep yore darn mouth shut, too. Never mind any singing."

He knew the well trained animal would not leave the clearing, and there was little chance of him getting an urge to neigh. Removing the bit and looping the reins, he left the horse contentedly cropping grass and slid into the growth. With the utmost care he worked his way toward where he had noted the smoke smudge. A couple of hundred yards of stealthy advance and the growth began to thin. Behind a final fringe he paused and peered cautiously forth.

Directly opposite, perhaps fifty yards distant, was a weather-beaten cabin, the former home, doubtless, of some wandering prospector. From the stick and mud chimney rose a trickle of smoke. Tied in front of the cabin were three saddled horses.

Crouched in the growth and safe from observation, Tom Carson pondered the situation. The cabin had a door and a window facing the brush in which he was concealed. Between the brush fringe and the building was open ground. On either side of the cabin and behind it the brush grew thickly.

" If I try to snuk across that clearing, I'm mighty liable to get me a dose of lead pizening," Carson mused. " If somebody happens to be looking out the window they can't miss seeing me. Wonder if that shack has a back door?"

He resolved to find out. Stealing through the growth he skirted the cabin and the clearing, crossing the trail a hundred yards above. Then he worked his way to the rear of the building. At a distance of only a few yards he peered forth.

There was a back door to the cabin, and it stood ajar. A path led from the door to where a little spring welled from the loam and sent a thread of water to join the main stream. Listening intently, Carson could hear the sound of voices within the cabin, but he could not make out what was being said.

He debated the feasibility of entering by the back door.

" But if those jiggers in there—and there are three of them at least—happen to be facing this way, there's a mighty slim chance of me getting the drop on them in time," he reasoned. " Nope, it's too risky."

For some minutes he lay silent, thinking hard.

" I've got to get their attention centred on the front of the house—on the clearing out there," he muttered.

Suddenly his eyes glowed with inspiration. He pushed back his broad brimmed hat and ruffled his thick black hair, as was a habit with him when satisfied with the solution of some problem. Then he cuffed the hat back over his right eye, turned and slipped swiftly through the growth until he reached the spot where he had left his horse. Here he immediately got busy. He collected twigs for a fire, got two forked sticks and drove them into the ground. Across the forks he laid a third stick, the upper side of which he carefully flattened with his knife. On this flat surface he laid four six-gun cartridges taken from his belt. Under the horizontal stick he heaped the twigs, the heap high at each end and hollowed out in the middle, and touched a match to them. They burned slowly, but soon the flames were licking at the horizontal crosspiece. With a final estimating glance at the slowly burning fire, he again slipped into the growth and circled the cabin to the rear. Only a few yards from the sagging back door he crouched intent and ready, his hands resting on the butts of his guns.

" When that cross stick burns through and dumps the shells into the fire, things ought to happen," he muttered, his eyes glued on the back door of the cabin.

Minutes passed, and nothing happened. He could hear the rumble of voices in the cabin, and an occasional stamp outside as one of the tethered horses protested against an inquisitive fly.

"Did that darn fire go out?" Carson asked himself. "That stick sure ought to have burned through by now."

He straightened a trifle from his cramped position, then jumped in spite of himself.

From across the clearing had sounded the bang of a gunshot. Another followed it, and another, in quick succession.

Carson heard the crash of an overturned chair, a clatter of boots on the wooden floor of the cabin. And at that instant the fourth cartridge let go.

Carson leaped from the growth and streaked for the back door. He crashed it wide open with his shoulder and dashed into the cabin. Three men who were peering excitedly through the front window whirled at his entrance. One was the man he had been trailing, the second was of similar appearance. The third was Jim Hill.

"Elevate!" Carson roared. "Yuh're covered!"

He took a step forward as the astounded trio started raising their hands. He stepped on a greasy tin plate that had fallen from the table. The plate slid under his feet. Carson reeled, floundered, and, as the plate skidded across the room, he lost his balance and fell.

Instantly the three men went for their guns; but even as he hit the floor, Carson dropped his left hand gun and seized a leg of the table in a convulsive grip. A mighty wrench and over went the table on its side, between Carson and the three gunmen. Carson grabbed up his fallen gun again and crouched low behind the table.

Bullets drummed against the table-top as the three opened fire; but the top was a slab of inch-and-a-half seasoned oak and the slugs did not pierce it.

Over the edge of the protecting table, Carson's Colts streaked fire. One of the Yaqui breeds gave a choking cough, staggered and fell. Bullets hammered the table-top and whistled over it. Carson shoved his Colts up again and pulled trigger. The second breed screamed shrilly, an animal howl of agony and terror, and pitched headlong. Carson chanced a glance over his protecting barrier just as Jim Hill's guns roared. With bullets knocking splinters from the table and storming over it, Carson lined sights with the outlaw. His finger squeezed the trigger.

And at that instant the world exploded in jagged flame and roaring sound. He heard the boom of his gun echo loudly in his ears, saw Hill reel back, blood spurting from his right forearm. Then the owlhoot whirled about, jerked the front door open and vanished, Carson's last wavering shot whining after him.

Through a fog of pain and whirling blackness, Carson dimly heard the clatter of speeding hoofs fading away from the cabin. Then the icy blackness closed over him, fold on clammy fold. His guns fell from his nerveless hands and he sprawled on his face to lie without sound or motion, blood slowly dripping from under his black hair to the floor.

Chapter 5

WHEN Carson finally regained his senses, he realized that he had been unconscious for many hours. The blood on his face was dry and caked; the fire had burned itself to ashes and the stove was cold; the sun was low in the west. He was wretchedly sick and weak from the terrific blow dealt him by the slug that has creased his scalp, but he managed to stagger to his feet.

The stiffened bodies of the Yaqui breeds lay sprawled in contorted positions. Carson surveyed them grimly.

" Well, for a jigger who is dedicated to the saving of life, I've sure been working in reverse of late! " he muttered.

But just the same he felt no qualm of conscience over the two vicious killers who lay dead on the cabin floor. The world had lost nothing by their passing, nor would it be any the worse off, Carson felt, if he succeeded in wiping out Jim Hill's entire band, including Hill himself.

There was a pot of coffee on the stove. Carson got the fire going and heated the coffee. After several steaming cups he felt somewhat better. He made his way to the spring in back of the cabin and washed the blood from his face. Then he went to look for his horse. He found the roan contentedly cropping grass in the little clearing by the stream. He got the rig off the cayuse and carried it to the cabin. Then he dressed and bandaged his creased head, dragged the two bodies outside, and proceeded to rustle some chuck, of which he was badly in need.

The cabin was stocked with provisions—evidently it had been used as a hangout for some time—and Carson threw a good meal together. It was nearly dark when he finished eating, He rolled a cigarette, smoked thoughtfully, and began to feel something like his normal self. He debated the advisability of spending the night in the cabin and decided that there was little or no chance of Hill returning at present.

"He'll need a job of bandaging done on that arm I punctured, and he won't be feeling over peart right now," he told himself with satisfaction. "He'll hole up somewhere for the night. Likely as not he's got more than one hangout in this blasted hole-in-the-wall section. Anyhow, I sure don't feel like ambling around right now. With chairs shoved against the doors, I figger I can take a chance."

He built up the fire, stretched out on a bunk that was built against the wall, and in a moment was fast asleep.

Dawn was breaking when Carson awoke. He was stiff and sore, but otherwise felt fit for anything. He cooked and ate breakfast, and by that time it was light enough to pick up Jim Hill's trail.

It led down the canyon and was easy to follow. Carson saddled his horse and again took up the chase.

Mile after mile he followed the track. He found where Hill had spent the night beneath the sheltered overhang of a cliff, and from various signs judged that the fugitive was not more than five hours ahead of him.

The canyon opened into another which trended due south. Soon Carson was convinced that he had crossed the Mexican Border. Ahead were mountains, a veritable ocean of peaks jutting up into the sky. The trail began to climb the slopes, and here it was harder to follow. Carson's speed was reduced to a snail's pace. At times he was forced to dismount and search for overturned pebbles, broken twigs or bent grass blades. At times he was at fault, but sooner or later he always picked up the track.

He climbed a long sag, the crest of which was thickly grown with low brush. Abruptly he reined in, staring westward into the sky.

Several miles distant, and almost due west of where he sat his horse, a tall, slender column of smoke was rising straight into the sky. It broke at its base, drifted slowly upward and dissipated in the limitless blue. Then up rolled an explosive ball. It was followed by another and another. Then a second long column poured into the sky. Then four tumbling balls in quick succession.

Carson stared at the dancing smoke balls with a darkening face. He knew very well what it meant. Somewhere over there in the brush an Indian was manipulating a blanket or deerskin over a brush fire. It was Indian smoke talk. Somebody was sending a message to somebody else. It might have nothing to do with himself, but then again it might. Carson swept the sky with his keen gaze.

Yes, there it was! Far to the south smoke was rising. He watched the puffs rise, vanish, be replaced by others. They ceased, and he turned his gaze westward once more.

Up from the brush streamed a single tall column. It broke, drifted upward, dissipated. The sky remained clear.

" Sent his message, got his answer, and signalled ' Okay '! " Carson muttered.

He tightened his grip on the reins and sent his horse down the long further slope. He reached the bottom and found himself in a narrow gorge. Directly in front was an almost cliff-like rise ending in a rounded crest. The bottom of the gorge was grown thickly with brush that came almost to the shoulders of a mounted man.

Staring at the crest, Carson suddenly crouched low in the saddle. From behind the crest a Yaqui Indian had floated noiselessly up against the sky, as if drawn upward by invisible wires. Clearly outlined against the blue of the sky, he stood staring into the gorge.

In the clear light no detail was lacking—fringed buckskins, deerskin band about the brows, binding down the lank black hair cut in a square bang, necklace of glittering stones, sheathed knife, long rifle cradled in the crook of his arm.

As Carson gazed, a second Yaqui face floated into view from behind the hilltop. A third appeared and a fourth.

For some minutes they remained in plain sight, staring down into the gorge. Then they turned, and vanished as mysteriously as they had come. Carson drew a long breath of relief.

" Didn't see me," he muttered. " If they had, they wouldn't have stood up there against the sky like that, easy marks for anybody down here.   The thing is, did they trail their ropes, or are they quietly camping over the other side of that ridge?"

For long minutes Carson remained in concealment; then as no more Indians appeared, he cautiously crossed the gorge.

Hill's trail led up the sag, and here it was easy to follow, for his scrambling horse had displaced stones and broken brush in its progress up the precipitous slope.

Under the lip of the rise, Carson dismounted. He stole forward, taking advantage of every bit of cover that offered, until he could peer over the crest.

Not an Indian was in sight.   The slope before him descended into a wide valley which stretched to another slope with a low, rounded crest that hinted of still another valley beyond. The valley was fully five miles in width.

After another long wait, Carson mounted once more and crossed the ridge.   The trail led across the valley in almost a straight line to the far slope.   At the bottom of the farther sag, he paused, casting a glance at the westering sun.

He estimated that it would be nearly full dark by the time he reached the rounded summit of the ridge, and he had no means of knowing what awaited him on the farther side. Besides, the weakness of the morning had returned and his wounded head throbbed painfully. He decided to camp in the valley for the night, and began casting about for a favourable spot.

Luckily he found a shallow recess in the face of a beetling ledge of rock.   After turning his horse loose to graze, he spread his blanket in the recess, kindled a tiny fire and proceeded to cook some supper.   The overhang of the crevice hid the light of his fire and the gathering dusk made its slight smoke invisible.   He ate with but little appetite, although he was sadly in need of food.   Then, blind with weariness and the ache in his head, he stretched out and went to sleep.

His sleep was the sodden unconsciousness of a drugged

man. He did not hear the inquiring snort of his horse standing in the shadow of the cliff, nor note its forward pricking ears as it gazed up the slope. The stars wheeled westward, changed from gold to silver. The east greyed and a wan light stole into the valley. Carson still slept, huddled in his blanket, and as he slept a ring of death closed silently around him.

Quietly, patiently, the fierce Yaqui warriors waited. They would not attack until the dawn, when their victim would be confused by the low, puzzling light. Patiently they waited until the first red spears of the morning shot zenithward. Then they rose from behind bush and rock, cocked rifles at the ready.

Tom Carson awoke suddenly with an undefinable sense of foreboding. He sat up in his blankets, and looked squarely into the muzzles of levelled rifles. Behind the steady barrels were dark, sinister faces and beady glittering eyes.

Slowly, Carson raised his hands shoulder high. To attempt to resist would be madness. The Yaquis had him covered with half a dozen guns. He was " caught settin'."

For a long moment his captors regarded him silently. Then one lowered his rifle and circled around until he could draw Carson's guns from under his saddle, which he had used for a pillow. Dark hard hands went over his body, feeling at the back of his neck for a possible knife, and under his armpits for a hidden gun. Satisfied that the captive was completely disarmed, the Yaqui stepped back with a guttural grunt. Then he spoke one word in Spanish.

" Come! "

With rifles levelled at his back, Carson followed his captor to where his horse was held. Another man brought his saddle and bridle, gesturing to Carson to get the rig on. He obeyed, and mounted at the Yaqui's order. His feet were deftly bound to the stirrups, his hands tied behind him. The Yaquis went through his saddlebags, eyed the medicine case suspiciously, fumbled the catch and opened it. They gave guttural grunts of pleasure at sight of the two shiny amputating knives, but would not touch the drugs or surgical implements. They closed the case and restored it to the saddlebag.

" Saving everything for the Chief, the chances are," Carson told himself.

Shaggy ponies were led from the brush. The Yaquis mounted. One took the bridle of Carson's horse and the little cavalcade started up the sag.

They crossed the ridge and before them lay, as Carson had suspected, another valley. Upon reaching the floor of this, they diagonalled across it, trending to the west. Carson saw, partly with regret, partly with thanksgiving, that Jim Hill's trail he had been following continued straight across the valley. He regretted the lost opportunity of catching up with the outlaw, but was thankful that, apparently at least, the band that had captured him was not part of Hill's outfit.

" With his gang, I'd have about as much show as a rabbit in a hounddog's mouth," he told himself. Mebbe I won't have any better with this outfit, but there's always a chance of something turning up."

Something was due to turn up, something utterly unexpected.

The Yaquis followed the valley for several miles. Then they climbed the slope and descended into still another valley. It was three or four miles and walled to the south by a beetling slope that swelled upward for several thousand feet. Half way up was a narrow cleft shut in by tall cliffs. For this cleft the Yaquis headed.

They reached it and entered the gloomy gorge, which wound away into the heart of the mountains. For fully five miles they followed the rugged chasm, their horses' hoofs echoing hollowly from the encroaching walls. Finally the cleft made an abrupt turn, the rock walls fell away and before them lay a wide amphitheatre level-floored and ringed about by hills. Another mile of riding and they passed through a grove and Carson perceived a cluster of well built huts and more Yaquis.

Surrounding the huts was good pasture dotted with clumps

of trees. Here grazed sizeable herds of cattle and goats and a number of horses.

As they approached the huts, it seemed to Carson that excitement prevailed in the little settlement. Men were running about and talking in front of a hut much larger than the others.

His captors sensed it too. One of them touched up his horse and rode on ahead. He dismounted and engaged a man in conversation. The news he received was evidently bad. The man talked excitedly, pointing to his own leg about halfway between the ankle and the knee. The other shook his head regretfully and stared at the big hut.

Carson's mind was working swiftly.

" Looks like somebody has been hurt," he told himself. " This may be a break for me."

They were almost up to the huts when a tall, lance-straight man whose black hair was sprinkled with grey came out. Carson could see that his face wore a strained expression. The man who had ridden ahead spoke to him, gesturing toward the captive. The tall man, who, Carson rightly suspected was the chief of the tribe, waved his hand impatiently and was turning to enter the hut when Carson shouted loudly in Spanish:

" Medico! Medico! "

The tall man halted, staring at Carson, then he strode up to him.

" You say you are a doctor?" he asked eagerly in excellent Spanish.

" I am," Carson replied.

Instantly the chief gutturalled an order to Carson's captors. They hastily cut the lashings that bound him to the stirrups, and freed his hands. The chief gestured him to dismount, which Carson did stiffly, rubbing his numb wrists.

" Come in," the chief said abruptly, and led the way to the hut.

The hut was comfortably furnished, more in Mexican than Yaqui style. Skin rugs covered the wooden floor. There were chairs, a mirror, a table and a bedstead.

Two women in the hut, bending over the couch opposite the bed, turned as Carson entered.

One was a middle-aged Yaqui woman. The other, much younger, Carson instantly saw was no Indian but a Mexican. She was good looking, with great black eyes, glossy black hair and red lips. Her regularly featured face was contorted with grief.

Lying on the couch was a half-breed boy of perhaps seven or eight years old. He was covered to the waist with a brightly coloured blanket.

The chief spoke to the younger woman. She turned eagerly to Carson.

" You are a doctor?" she asked quickly.

" Si, Señora," Carson replied.

The woman clasped her hands. Then she gestured to the boy on the couch.

" Our son," she said. " He is terribly injured. Half an hour ago he went too close to a young horse that had just been driven in and it kicked him. His leg—it is fearfully broken!"

Tears rolled down her cheeks, and again she clasped her slender fingers together until they whitened.

" Can—can you do anything for him? " she asked appealingly.

Carson moved to the couch and carefully turned back the blanket. His lips pursed in a soundless whistle. The boy's leg was not only broken, the bone was completely smashed. A splintered end protruded through the skin.

The chief, who was evidently the boy's father, looked questioningly at Carson. The girl wept convulsively.

" Must he die? " the chief asked in low tones.

" No reason I can see for his dying," Carson replied, " but I can't save his leg. It'll hafta be amputated."

An expression of horror crossed the father's face.

" Cut off his leg! " he ejaculated. " What's the use of living with only one leg? "

" Plenty of use," Carson replied. " He's young and has his whole life before him. In a couple weeks he'll be hobbling around on crutches, and not long after that he could use a peg that you or I could make him and get around fine. You speak Spanish, Chief, and yuh evidently have been to Mexican towns. You know cork legs can be made for folks that have lost one of their own. With one of those and wearing boots, nobody would know he'd ever lost a leg."

" Yes, yes!" the girl exclaimed. " I have seen them. Quijano, the doctor is right."

" And he'll die if the leg isn't cut away? " the chief asked.

" Certain to," Carson replied. " It isn't a simple break, yuh see; the bone is all smashed and splintered and thrust through the flesh. It's a compound fracture and a bad one. If it isn't taken off, mortification will set in soon and he'll die. It's the only chance, Chief."

"And you think he will live if you take off the leg?"

" Got a mighty good chance to," Carson replied. " He's mighty nigh dead from shock right now; there is very little life in him; but if he doesn't die of shock, I'm sure the operation won't kill him. He's spent his whole life in the open, I figure, and he oughta be hard as nails. I really believe he'll come through it all right. Anyhow, he's sure to die if nothing is done."

" It shall be tried," the chief said abruptly. " Why shouldn't it be, when a medico is brought to my village now of all times. The padres at the Mission, who taught me Spanish, also taught of a God who did things for people. I never believed in Him, but now I'm beginning to wonder. A medico, at this moment! What do you wish me to do? "

Carson looked at the child. He lay with his eyes half closed, without a vestige of colour in his cheeks.

" Give him some warm milk with a spoonful of aguardiente in it. Do this at once. He is prostrated by shock and I want to build him up a little."

The attendant at once hurried to prepare the milk. Carson turned to the chief again.

" My medicine and instrument case is in the saddlebags," he said. " I'll need them."

E

The chief hurried to the door and called an order. A few minutes later, Carson's riding gear, guns and other belongings were carried in and, by direction of the chief, deposited on the table. Carson opened the instrument case and took forth the amputation knives and other needful articles.

" Now I want a large jug of warm water, a bowl and some soft rags," he told the Yaqui. " Also a couple of small flat stones with rounded edges, a strip of soft skin, and a bit of stick three or four inches long and as thick as your finger, to make a tourniquet with. I think that will be all."

The requested materials were quickly provided. Carson abruptly addressed the chief again.

" Have yuh by any chance a fine saw?" he asked.

The chief shook his head.

Carson's black brows drew together. Here suddenly was a problem.

" I've got to have something to cut through the bone with," he said. These knives are fine for the flesh cut, but what I'm going to do about the bone I don't know."

He fingered the knife thoughtfully as he spoke. Suddenly he had an inspiration.

"Give me a hand," he told the chief. " Hold this knife steady on the table with the cutting edge uppermost. That's right. Now I'll see what I can do. This knife is of the very best steel—much like a razor's steel—and yuh know the least thing will notch a razor."

He drew forth his pocket knife as he spoke, and opened it. Then he began to carefully nick the cutting edge of the amputating knife with the blade of the pocket knife. Ten minutes' work and the job was done.

" Now get me a piece of fresh bone," he directed.

The bone was soon forthcoming and Carson found that his improvised saw cut through it very cleanly.

" This will do fine," he said. "The operation is the most simple in surgery, so long as yuh have the proper tools. We oughtn't to have a bit of trouble. Let's take a look at the boy, now."

Carson found to his satisfaction that the warm milk had already done its work. The boy was perfectly conscious and there was a slight colour in his cheeks. His pulse had gained strength wonderfully. Carson nodded approvingly to the chief.

" He'll do," he said. " Now let's get to work."

From the medicine case he took a small bottle of chloroform and regarded it dubiously.

"A mighty little bit for a job like this," he said, " but it will hafta do."

He quickly instructed the attendant, a stolid and capable Yaqui woman whose nerves were not the least affected by the tragedy, how to administer the anæsthetic. His instructions were received with a nod of understanding and a phlegmatic grunt.

" Tell the boy I am going to do him good," he instructed the mother. " Tell him not to move or resist, and to do just as he is told. All right, let's go."

A few minutes later Carson lifted one of the child's eyelids; the eye was turned upward, so that the iris was no longer visible.

" He's gone off," Carson said. " Now for the tourniquet. That's right, Chief, twist it gradually, now, and place the flat stone on the main artery—right there. Hold the stick firm with one hand and place the other on his chest. I don't think he'll move, but we can't take chances. Lay your arm across him," he told the mother; " that's right. Kneel with yore face against his. Grasp the leg just below the knee and hold it right," he directed the attendant.

Carson gripped the amputating knife firmly and bent over the injured member. A moment later he uttered a low exclamation of satisfaction. The flesh was cut through and no cry had escaped the child. He had not struggled in the least. Another instant the foot and the lower portion of the leg came away at the point where the bone was crushed. Carson pushed the flesh upward so as to expose another inch or so of the shin-bone. Working swiftly so as to forestall the lessening effect of the meagre dose of chloroform, he cut through the bone with the saw. With a strand of silk and needle he took up the ends of the arteries and tied them with the silk. He loosened the tourniquet a trifle, and nodded with satisfaction; the arteries were securely tied. He tightened it again and gave it to the chief to hold. He wiped the wound with a damp cloth, drew down the flesh over the end of the bone, brought up the flap of flesh from behind and with a few stitches sewed it in its place. The ends of the threads that tied the arteries were left hanging out of the wound. When the superfluous tips of the main arteries, below the ties, had rotted away, the threads would be drawn out. It would be some days, however, before the ligatures were free.

Carson straightened his aching back.

"All done," he said. "He'll be coming around before long, now. When he does, tell him he will be well soon, but now he must go back to sleep."

He stood watching until the child drowsily opened his eyes. His mother spoke softly to him, and with a faint smile he closed his eyes again. Carson waited another moment.

"He's asleep now," he told the chief. "Yuh don't need to hold him any longer. Have some warm milk ready and give it to him when he wakes up. Don't tell him about having his foot taken off, and keep a blanket over him so he won't see what's been done. Tell him he mustn't move his leg or it'll hurt him. Two or three weeks and he'll be hobbling around on crutches."

Tears were running down the old chief's face. His wife was sobbing with joy. The chief gripped Carson's hand, while the mother clung to the other.

"Señor, what can I do to repay you?" the chief asked brokenly.

"Well," chuckled Carson, "right now a little breakfast would come in handy. Yore boys were in such a hurry to have me visit with them this morning that I didn't stop to cook any."

In the pure, dry mountain air, the little patient made rapid progress toward recovery. When the time came to remove the ligatures, they came gliding out of the healing tissues as easily as snakes from their holes. A little trickle of pus followed, only slightly tinged with blood. Carson breathed with relief. The arteries had not burst; all the wound needed now was the free drainage open to it with the withdrawal of the ligatures.

" Fine!" he told the chief, who was eyeing the drainage with concern. " That flow is what is known as ' laudable pus '; it's just the drainage from a wound cleanly healing itself. Yuh'll notice it has but a faint odour of corruption. The ooze from a gangrened limb is much stronger and very unpleasant. Now we don't have a thing to worry about."

The three weeks that followed passed pleasantly enough, although Carson was impatient to get back to Tombstone. He rode with the chief and his young men, hunted and fished. And he and the chief had long talks which Carson found extremely interesting.

" I went to school and was taught by the padres of the San Vicente Mission," he told Carson. " I learned to speak Spanish and learned, also, the white man's ways. I decided they were not good for my people, so I came back to the tribe of which my father was chief, and of which, in the course of time I became chief. I resolved that the ways of the white men were not for my people, and ordered it thus. My young men hunt and fish, tend their herds and till the soil as their fathers did before the Spaniards came to this land. They are healthy, happy and free. They live upright, simple lives and are content, which they would not be in the white man's settlements. The Mexicans hate us, but they leave us alone, for we are strong and we can fight. This village is one of several hidden here in the mountain fastnesses. Together we can put many fighting men to the defence of our people. We do not allow strangers to stop here in our mountains. That is why my young men took you. You were seen riding this way, and watched."

Carson nodded and rolled a cigarette.

"Reckon that's what the smoke talk I saw was about," he commented.

The chief nodded in reply, smiling slightly as he accepted a smoke from the white medico.

"Yes," he said, "the word was sent thus to those who waited. They could have killed you, but I do not allow the killing of strangers who give no offence. Only in defence of our rights do we kill. You would have been sent away with a warning, or, if we thought wise, kept a prisoner, perhaps for a long period."

Carson could understand this, and he was more than ever thankful for the opportunity to do the grim old Yaqui a favour that made him his friend. It was not pleasant to contemplate captivity here in the desolate mountains, maybe for years. He had heard of such things.

During his stay with the Yaquis, Carson revised some of his opinions concerning the mountain fighters. He learned they were not naturally the dour, taciturn folks he had observed in the towns and settlements north of the Line. They could be gay and talkative, and liked to laugh and play jokes on one another. Their tribal dances were sprightly and well done. They were hospitable; their family ties were close; and they were intensely loyal to their chief.

The chief's wife, he learned, was a Mexican girl of good family whom he had met in the course of one of his visits to the Mission. She seemed perfectly content with her life of solitude, and her gratitude to Carson for saving the life of her child was boundless.

Carson frankly told the chief what brought him into the mountains.

The old warrior looked grave at the mention of Jim Hill.

"I have heard of the man," he said. "He is a muy malo hombre. He has gathered companions as evil as he, though lacking his cunning. It is a dangerous task you have set yourself, amigo. Better far to abandon the quest!"

But Tom Carson's jaw set grimly, he was silent.

Another week and the chief's son was walking about the hut on crutches Carson made for him. His father was planning a trip to Mexico City to procure an artificial limb as soon as the healing of the stump would make its use possible.

" It's time for me to go now," Carson told the chief. " Yuh don't need me any longer and I'm anxious to get back to Tombstone."

The old chief gazed long and earnestly at the young doctor, hesitated, seemed to arrive at a sudden decision.

" And you still pursue the man Hill? " he asked.

Carson nodded, his face grim.

" My young men have learned things about the man," the Chief said. " They tracked him eastward from where you left his trail. They learned that he is in Hildalgo county, New Mexico. A band of outlaws is operating there, with a tall, black-eyed stranger at their head. I doubt not it is the man you seek. So if you must continue the pursuit——"

" Thanks for putting me on the right track," Carson interrupted. " Okay, I'm headed for New Mexico. Adios, Chief."

" Come to see us when you can," the chief urged him. " Here you will always be welcome. ' Vaya usted con Dios, amigo! '—Go you with God, friend! "

Chapter 6

SHERIFF BOB MATHERS sat in his office talking with his chief deputy, Dave Wilson. Mathers was a big bulky man with a good-humoured smile, and was generally liked. Wilson was lean, nervous, cantankerous, but had the reputation of being a first class peace officer.

Wilson suddenly cocked his head sideways in a listening attitude.

" Somebody headed this way, and comin' fast," he remarked.

Mathers nodded, and continued to stuff tobacco into his old black pipe. He glanced inquiringly over the bowl of the pipe as the door flung open and a man dashed in, breathing hard, his eyes wild with apprehension.

" Sheriff! " he gulped, " the Harlow brothers and their hands are in the Ace-Full saloon, drunk and raisin' hell. And there's another big jigger, a stranger, with them. Looks tough! Yuh'd better hightail down there before a killin' comes off."

With a disgusted snort, Sheriff Mathers fished his gun belt from a drawer and buckled it on. Wilson, who removed his gun only when he removed his pants, did not have to reach for it. He merely stood up, stretched his long arms and yawned.

" Okay," grunted the sheriff, " let's go, Dave."

When they reached the Ace-Full, they found it a bedlam. Tables were overturned, chairs smashed. A man with his head split open lay on the floor. A bartender, a dazed look in his eyes, sagged against the back bar and mopped shakily at his bloody face with a towel.

At the far end of the bar, in a tight group, stood the Harlow brothers, Sime and Wesley, and five of their hands. There was also a man Mathers had never seen. He was tall, bulky and had a black beard and glittering black eyes.

The sheriff took one look at the carnage, and his face set grimly.

"All right, you hellions," he called to the Harlows. "Yuh're goin' to the calaboose."

For an instant there was silence; then the rooms seemed to fairly explode with the roar of sixshooters.

Sheriff Mathers staggered back, vainly trying to draw his gun. Wilson's hand flashed down and up.

"Look out for Dave Wilson!" Wesley Harlow yelled.

Just as Wilson pulled trigger, the tall stranger turned sideways to him. The cool action in the thick of the furious tumult of battle was characteristic of iron-nerved Jim Hill. Wilson's bullet fanned his face instead of drilling him dead centre.

Throwing open his coat Hill seized a sawed-off shotgun hanging in a loop to his right shoulder, tipped it up and fired both barrels at Wilson.

The heavy double charge of buckshot lifted Wilson clean off his feet and crashed him sideways to the floor in a limp huddle. Jim Hill let his shotgun swing back on its shoulder band beneath his coat, snapped his Colt from its holster and fired twice at the staggering sheriff.

Ten seconds after he had entered the saloon, ten seconds of the smoke of blazing guns, packed with murderous hatred and flaming death, Sheriff Mathers reeled out onto the street and sank to the ground, both arms broken, his body shot through and through, with only minutes to live.

Stepping over the body of Deputy Dave Wilson who lay with his face buried in the sawdust, the Harlows and Jim Hill left the saloon with drawn guns. Nobody tried to stop them.

Nobody tried to stop them when they mounted their horses and clattered out of town and were lost in the darkness of a moonless night.

As they raced across the star-burned prairie, young Wesley Harlow drew up alongside his towering, broad-shouldered brother and Jim Hill!

"Sime," he said, "we-uns killed a sheriff and his dep'ty. We're on the run now."

Sime Harlow's eyes flashed. "Well, what the hell of it?" he growled.

"Sime," Wesley persisted, "we-uns will need money, and we ain't got none."

"Okay," Jim Hill answered for the elder Harlow, "we'll get some."

"How?"

"You foller me and stop askin' damphool questions and yuh'll see. I've had somethin' in mind ever since I coiled my twine here for a spell a coupla months back. Reckon it's about time to pull it off. Close yore trap and ride."

For another mile they rode in silence, the Harlows and Hill in the lead, the five Rocking H cowboys herding close behind.

Jim Hill abruptly slowed the pace. A moment later he turned into a rutted track that branched from the main trail.

"Up here a quarter of a mile is the Preston stone quarry," he said. "They got somethin' up there we'll need. Foller my lead, now, and keep yore eyes skun."

The shadow cutting of the quarry hove into view. The buildings were dark, but a single light burned in a little shanty set off to one side.

Outside the shanty Hill dismounted. He strode to the door, his man close behind him, and flung it open.

Inside the shanty, the lone watchman on the job leaped to his feet as the Harlows crowded through the door, hats drawn low over their glinting eyes.

"What the hell do you fellers want?" demanded the watchman, and half turned to a rifle that leaned against the wall nearby.

Jim Hill's answer was to lace two bullets through his heart.

"Get his keys and pack his lantern along, too," he told young Wesley.

Leaving the shanty he led the way to a small building set at some distance from the other structures. It was painted a flaming red and plastered with signs reading "Danger."

Hill found the right key and fitted it into the lock. He threw open the door, took the lantern and, holding it in front of him gingerly stepped into the powder house.

"A dozen sticks had oughta be plenty," he said, indicating the boxes of greasy looking dynamite cylinders. "Take a coil of fuse and some caps. Careful how yuh handle that stuff. If it goes off we'll have a damn long drop to take before we land in hell. Okay, let's get out of here. Wrap that powder in yore coat, Wes, and be easy with it. Let's go. We ain't got no time to waste."

They left the quarry and followed the track back to the main trail. Along this they rode swiftly for half an hour, then Jim Hill turned sharply to the south and rode across the prairie until the twin steel ribbons of the C & P Railroad glimmered in the starlight.

Along the line of the railroad he led his men, until he drew rein beside a short trestle that spanned the wash.

The outlaws dismounted. Hill eased down the bank of the wash until he could reach where the girders that held the rails rested on the stonework of the pier.

"Pass down that dynamite." he told Wesley. "Hang onto a coupla sticks; we may need 'em for somethin' else."

He capped a fuse, crimped it to one of the dynamite sticks and tied the sticks together with a torn neckerchief.

"Okay," he said, squatting on the bank and rolling a cigarette. "You fellers lead the horses back inter the brush and hole up there. Get far enough back so yuh won't get blowed to hell when this stuff let's go."

"Yuh got that fuse cut awful damn short, Jim," said young Wesley peering by the uncertain light of the watchman's lantern.

"You 'tend to yore own knittin'," the other snarled at him. "Get the hell inter the brush with them horses. I know what I'm doin'."

Squatting silently on the bank, the outlaw watched until he saw the gleam of an approaching headlight round a curve a mile distant. With narrowed eyes he watched it draw nearer, calculating the speed of its approach. With a steady hand he held the glowing end of his lighted cigarette to the fuse.

The Chevalier, one of the C & P's crack transcontinental passenger trains, was late and making up time. In the cab, the old engineer sat with one hand on the throttle bar, the other toying with the handle of his airbrake valve. His glance along the track ahead was perfunctory, for here the steel ran over the level prairie, arrow-straight for several miles, with no danger of slides or falling rocks. He glanced at his watch, frowned, and widened the throttle a trifle. The stack of the great locomotive chuckled a quicker song. The spinning drivers hummed against the rails, their monotonous grind punctuated by the clang and clatter of the flashing side rods.

A red glare filled the cab as the fireman flung open the fire door and bailed " black diamonds " into the roaring inferno of the firebox. A " squirrel tail " of steam rose lazily from the safety valve. The needle of the steam gauge wavered against the two hundred mark. Black smoke belched from the purring stack. The door clanged shut and the fireman hopped back to his seatbox and leaned out of the window, blinking his eyes to free them from the glare of the fire.

Ahead, a line of black shadow split the prairie. It was a deep and narrow wash. The steel cut the gloom of the wash with straight ribbons that shimmered like silver in the beam of the headlight. The trestle was but a few hundred yards ahead of the speeding train.

From the black gulf of the wash torrented a sheet of yellow flame. A crashing thunder drowned the clang of steel on steel and the rumbling roar of the heavy train. The gleaming ribbons of the track vanished into nothingness in a cloud of smoke.

The engineer tried to save his train, but he didn't have a chance. He slammed the throttle shut, " wiped the gauge " with his airbrake handle.

But even as the air screeched from the cylinders and the shoes ground against the tyres, the engine struck the twisted rails and bent girders that had spanned the wash. With a shattering roar it plunged into the depths. The baggage car followed it, piling end-on on top of it. The express car slammed into the up-ended baggage car, bounced, rocked, left the rails and plowed deep into the soft soil, coming to a halt with one end overhanging the wash. Half the coaches behind were derailed, the remainder jammed and battered.

From the dark gulf which was the grave of the engineer, the fireman and the baggage master, arose a bellow of escaping steam. Through it knifed the screams of injured and terrified passengers.

The doors of the express car were wrenched wide open and jammed in their slots by the terrific impact. Toward the open door, next to them, guns out and ready, rushed the Harlow outfit.

Flame spurted from the express car. One of the outlaws cursed as a bullet seared his shoulder. The others dropped to the ground and sought cover.

" I'll fix the skunks," growled Jim Hill, and puffed hard on his still lighted cigarette.

Something soared into the air from where he lay, something that left a trail of sparks behind it. It vanished through the open door of the express car.

Again there was a crashing explosion. Smoke boiled from the open door. The outlaws waited a moment for the smoke to clear, then cautiously got to their feet. No shots greeted them from the door.

"Fan out, you hellions, and shoot anybody what tries to come over this way from the train," Hill ordered his men. " Come on, Sime."

A single light that had not been extinguished by the explosion showed one messenger lying dead on the floor. The second, his face covered with blood sagged dazedly against the wall.

Jim Hill clambered into the car and shook him roughly. " All right," he growled, " open the safe."

" G-go to hell! " gasped the messenger.

Without wasting a word in argument, Hill shot him through the left arm.

" Now open it, while yuh can still use the other hand," he told the moaning man.

The messenger quailed beneath the outlaw's terrible glare. He staggered to the tall steel safe in one end of the car and twirled the combination knob with trembling fingers.

Outside sounded a shot echoed by a scream of pain. Hill did not even turn around. He watched the messenger twirl the knob until the tumblers clicked into place. Then he roughly shoved the man aside, seized the knob and swung the safe door open. He passed bags of clinking gold pieces to Wesley and Sime.

" Dump 'em out the door and whoop to some of the boys to come get 'em," he told his companions.

Five minutes later the outlaws sped away from the wrecked train with their loot.

And thus began the Hill and Harlow reign of terror in Hidalgo county.

Chapter 7

SWEATING and steaming under the blazing New Mexico sun, the Tree L trail herd rolled northward toward the shipping town of Martin. Old Lafe Sanderson, owner of the Tree L rode with a watchful eye on his big herd and for the surrounding country.

" We'll make it to Talkin' Water canyon to bed down for the night," he told his foreman. "Then we'll get an early start in the mawnin' and shove 'em on to town by noon."

" Yeah, Talkin' Water canyon is a safe place," agreed Clate Gray, the foreman. " And. yuh can't be too safe now-a-days, with the Harlows and them sidewinders swaller-forkin' all over the county."

" Somethin's gotta be done about them damn Harlows," growled Sanderson. " Sheriff Bulkley has about as much chance with that outfit as a wax dog chasin' a firebrick cat through hell. Shove 'em along, Clate, it's gettin' late."

Far in the rear of the herd, Dishonest Abe Strealey, the cook, rocked on the high seat of his lumbering chuck wagon. He put on the brakes as the big groanin' cart lurched down a grade to where, at the bottom of the hollow, a much narrower trail wound out of the brush and cut across the main track. It had rained the day before and the bottom of the hollow was muddy.

The wagon made it down the sag all right and started across the level. Without warning a rear wheel sank deep into a hole and stuck. The wagon brought up short, the bronks snorting, the driver cursing.

Dishonest Abe spoke to his horses in no uncertain terms, telling them to " git up and git this mess the hell outa here."

The horses were willing, but despite their most strenuous efforts, the wagon stayed where it was, the sunken rear wheel, slipping and sliding against the steep side of the hole.

Old Abe got down stiffly from his perch.   From the coonie, the sagging sheet of rawhide stretched and lashed to the running gear of the wagon, and used to carry firewood, he took a slab which he shoved under the wheel as far as he could.   Then he whooped to his horses, who again did their best, to no avail.   Abe tried to shove the slab under the tyre so it would provide a purchase for the turning wheel, but his strength was not equal to the task.   The horses surged against the traces, the wagon creaked and groaned, and stayed right where it was.

The old cook wiped his streaming brow, sat down on a boulder by the side of the trail, and talked for five minutes, and did not repeat himself.   He paused with his mouth hanging open, a particularly choice objurgation bit in two.

Behind him had sounded a mirthful chuckle.   As he turned a voice spoke.

"Would sound better set to music, don't yuh figger?"

Old Abe gawked at the speaker, who had ridden out of the brush unheard on the soft earth of the side trail.

He was a tall man, over six feet, wide of shoulder, lean of waist and hip.   He had a lean, bronzed face with a high-bridged nose, a rather wide mouth, grin quirked at the corners, a jutting chin and long, level grey eyes in the depths of which seemed to lurk a dancing devil of laughter.   The hair that showed beneath his pushed-back " J.B." was thick and crisp, and so black a blue shadow seemed to lie upon it.   He wore regulation range garb of overalls, batwing chaps, soft blue shirt, vivid handkerchief looped carelessly about his sinewy throat, and well scuffed, high-heeled boots of softly tanned leather.   Encircling his waist were double cartridge belts, and from the carefully worked and oiled hand-made holsters suspended from the belts protruded the black butts of heavy guns. He forked a magnificent roan horse.

"Yeah, mebbe if yuh used music on 'er, she'd roll," he chuckled.   "Like this:"

He threw back his black head, and a deep, rich voice pealed forth:

> " *Roll along, wagon-wheel, roll along,*
> *Take me back home where I belong;*
> *Biscuits in the oven, beans in the pot,*
> *Bacon in the fryin' pan, coffee steamin' hot.*"

Old Abe glowered at him.

" Think yuh're smart, don't cha! " he grunted disgustedly. " Yuh wouldn't feel so peart if yuh had twenty hungry cowhands waitin' for supper, and supper gonna be late! "

The tall stranger chuckled at the irate oldtimer. Then he swung lightly to the ground and inspected the offending wheel.

" I figger we can get er' out," he announced cheerfully. He uncoiled his rope, noosed the end of the wagon tongue and tied hard and fast to his saddle.

" Okay, Rojo, tighten 'er up," he told the roan horse, who obediently moved ahead on the trail until the sagging rope was taut.

He stepped back and again surveyed the sunken wheel.

" Be ready to shove the chunk under when I lift 'er," he told the cook.

" What yuh gabbin' about! " scoffed old Abe. " Two men couldn't lift that wheel outa that rut."

" Reckon they couldn't," the other agreed cheerfully ; " they'd be gettin' in each other's way. Let's go, now."

He gripped the hub of the wheel with both sinewy hands. Old Abe saw the seams of his well worn shirt stretch to the bursting point as great muscles leaped out on his arms and shoulders. Before the cook's astounded eyes, the ponderous wheel rose out of the rut until it was level with the surface of the trail. Mechanically he shoved the slab under it. The stranger eased the wheel down until the tyre was resting on the slab. He stepped back and straightened up, dusting his hands off.

" Give yore horses their powders, now," he directed.

Old Abe whooped to his bronks. The stranger's voice rang out also—

" Trail, Rojo! "

F

The roan lunged forward in unison with the wagon horses. The taut rope hummed like a harp string. The wagon moved ahead, reached solid ground.

" Hold it, Rojo! " the tall man called.

" Reckon that did it," he observed as he walked toward the wagon tongue to loosen his twine. Old Abe trudged beside him regarding him with awed eyes.

Abruptly the stranger halted, staring across the slackened rope.

Unobserved, three men had ridden across the open prairie to the left. At the far edge of the trail they sat their horses, interestedly observing operations.

One a little in advance of his companions was tall and lanky, with abnormally long arms and wide shoulders. He had a youthful face that was already deeply lined with the marks of dissipation. He had wild, reckless eyes set deep in cavernous sockets. At the moment those eyes were resting avidly on the magnificent roan horse.

Old Abe gulped in his throat as his glance ran over the man's face. He wet his suddenly dry lips with the tip of a nervous tongue.

The horseman turned his hot gaze back to the tall stranger. He spoke, in a harsh, growling voice.

" Cowboy," he said, " I sorta fancy that red hoss. S'pose yuh get the rig off him. You and me are gonna make a little swap."

As he spoke, he flashed a gun from its holster.

Old Abe could never explain satisfactorily, even to himself, just what happened or how.

There was a flicker of lean, sinewy hands, the crash of a shot and the horseman reeled in his saddle with a yelp of pain, blood streaming from his right hand. His gun, its lock smashed and battered, lay in the dust a dozen feet distant.

His companions streaked for their guns, then froze with them still leathered. They were looking into two unwavering black muzzles, one of them still wisping smoke, that yawned hungrily at them; and behind those rock-steady muzzles were two terrible cold eyes from which all the laughter had vanished.

" Never seed such eyes," old Abe told it later. " They was the colour of polished steel on a cold mawnin', and back in 'em were little crawling flickers like fire under ice. Give me the creeps up and down my backbone to look at 'em."

The stranger spoke, and his voice was no longer musically drawling. It was hard, brittle, like ice grinding under an iron tyre.

" Don't reach for the other one," he warned the wounded man. " I might miss my next shot, and when I ' miss ' it's allus inside a gent's gun hand."

The horseman understood even if he did not appreciate the grim jest. Neither he nor his companions laboured under any delusions as to where that next bullet would strike when it ' missed.' He gasped, glared, his eyes watering with rage, his face drawn and contorted with mad passion until it was like to a grotesque death mask. Twice he tried to speak, but the words seemed to choke in his throat. Finally he got them out, thick with menace.

" This—this ain't the last of it. I'll be seein' yuh again, damn yuh! "

" Look good the fust time, and look quick," the other replied imperturbably. " Yuh might not have time to look twice. All right, now, turn those cayuses and high tail back the way yuh come. Get goin'! "

The last words shot out like bullets and the unsavoury trio winced under their impact. Speechless, but with black glares of hatred, they turned their horses.

The tall, black-haired man holstered one gun and walked to his horse, his eyes never leaving them. He slid a heavy Winchester from where it snugged in the saddle boot and cradled it in his arms.

" This saddle gun is a coupla inches longer in the barrel than the ones you are packing," he remarked pointedly; " so don't make no mistakes. I've got the range on yuh."

There was no answer to the warning. Cruelly spurring

their horses, the three rode off at a gallop. The tall man holstered his second Colt and watched them until they vanished over a distant ridge.

Old Abe was regarding him with frightened eyes.

"Son," he said, his voice a trifle unsteady, "fork that red hoss of yores and hightail outa this section as fast as he can pack yuh. That was Wesley Harlow yuh winged."

"That so?" the other replied. "And just who is Wesley Harlow?"

Strealey stared.

"Yuh ain't from this section, eh?" he observed.

"Nope," the other replied. "Rode over here from the west."

"Wes Harlow is Sime Harlow's kid brother," old Abe said. "The Harlows and a big black-eyed sidewinder and their gang are the saltiest pack of hyderphobia skunks this section ever coughed up. They're plumb cultus and they don't fergit. They'll be on yore tail for this day's work, son. You trail the hell outa here—fast."

The other shook his head.

"Nope, reckon not," he replied. My horse is sorta fagged and don't feel up to skalleyhootin' right now."

Strealey glanced at the red horse, who was bright of eye, his coat satiny, his pose bespeaking boundless energy held in leash with difficulty.

"Yeah, so I notice," the cook remarked dryly. "Son, yuh're a plumb damphool; but I sorta cotton to yore kind of fool. My name's Strealey. Abe Strealey. Old Abe Strealey. I was named for 'Honest Abe' Lincoln, but folks with notions of bein' funny kinda changed it to Dishonest Abe, and I've sorta got used to it after packin' it for sixty years."

The other chuckled, and held out his hand. "Mine's Carson," he returned. "Front handle's got whittled down to Tom. Glad to know yuh Abe."

"And now," he added after they shook hands, "s'pose we get this shebang movin' 'fore those hungry punchers of yores plumb swell up and bust from too much wind pudding."

Chapter 8

THE story of what happened at the trail forks lost nothing in Abe Strealey's telling of it when they reached where the Tree L outfit had bedded down the trail herd. Grizzled Old Man Sanderson shook hands solemnly with Tom Carson.

"But what Abe handed out was good advice," he agreed. "Gettin' the Harlows down on yuh is bad business, son."

"But if yuh're in the notion of hangin' around a spell, I can use another tophand," he added.

"Might as well give it a whirl, I reckon," Carson replied. "My twine is sorta running loose right at the minute."

The Tree L hands had chosen the mouth of a narrow box canyon for the bedding ground. To the west the canyon wall was sheer, a beetling rampart of stone towering hundreds of feet into the air. To the east it was a slope so steep and rocky as to be practically unclimbable. This slope, after slanting upward for a couple of hundred yards, ended in a wide bench that jutted against the east wall of the canyon and tumbled over the ragged south end of the bench in a series of falls before it reached the prairie and flowed swiftly by east to join the Rio Grande.

"She runs out of a hole in the box end wall of the gulch," Lafe Sanderson told Carson, jerking his head toward the tumbling water. "This is a prime spot to bed a herd, with times like they are. They can't nobody come down the canyon, or down the side walls either. And we can keep a eye on the mouth. Which is somethin', with outfits like the Harlows runnin' loose. I ain't scairt, so long as they can't get the jump on me. Got twenty hands, and they're loaded for bear. About twice as many as I'd need to trail a herd of this size under ord'nary conditions."

Carson had already noticed the unusual size of the outfit,

one cowboy to every two hundred cattle or so being the normal ratio. In this instance it was doubled.

" Folks must be sorta jumpy hereabouts, all right," he mused as he attended to Rojo's wants. " Uh-huh, that black-eyed jigger Strealey spoke about is Jim Hill, all right."

The canyon was well grass grown and the tired beefs contentedly cropped and munched while the hungry punchers did ample justice to Dishonest Abe's offerings. The Tree L hands had pitched their camp near the mouth of the canyon and at some little distance from the boulder strewn slope. The canyon was so narrow and the cliffs that hemmed it in so high that the beetling west wall seemed to overhang the site of the camp. A little stretch of rocky, broken ground protected the camp from the possibility of a sudden stampede by the cattle. If such an unexpected happening did occur, the herd would be forced to circle the camp on their way out of the gorge.

Not that Sanderson feared or anticipated such an occurrence. But he posted more than the usual number of night hawks to ride herd on the beefs during the hours of darkness.

After filling themselves as full as possible with food and steaming coffee, the tired waddies spread their blankets and turned in. Soon the camp was quiet, save for the contented rumbling of the full fed and sleepy cattle, and the song, or what passed for it, of the night hawks slowly riding their monotonous rounds. An occasional mutter of distant thunder drifted from the west, but the sky was not heavily overcast and the chance of rain appeared slight.

But if there was peace in the Tree L trail camp, there was far from it in the abandoned prospector's cabin some miles to the west and south, which the Harlow gang was using for a temporary hangout.

Wesley Harlow, his bullet furrowed hand in a bandage, strode about muttering curses, his eye glaring with maniacal fury. The giant Sime slumped in a chair before the fire, his long legs stretched out, puffing at his pipe, apparently deep in thought and paying little mind to Wesley's tantrums, casting an occasional gruff remark at Jim Hill, who was brooding on the other side of the fireplace.

Suddenly, however, he whirled in his chair to glower at his brother.

" Shet up," he told him harshly. " Reckon yuh got what was comin' to yuh. Some day yuh'll get us all inter trouble with yore damphool stunts. Yuh got a good horse. What'd yuh wanta try and do a plumb stranger outa his for? Sometime, if yuh ever get anythin' but hair under yore hat, yuh'll larn to find out somethin' about strangers 'fore yuh jump em. Yuh're jest like damphools who have been knowed to pick up black diamond rattlers thinkin' they was bull snakes, and not takin' the trouble to find out for shore. By the way, what did that jigger what made yuh looklike a snail climbin' a slick log look like? "

One of the men who had accompanied Wes Harlow answered the question.

" Big tall, wide-shouldered jigger, over six feet," he said. " Black hair, grey eyes that seemed to go through yuh like a greased bullet. Sort of a hawk nose. Packed two guns."

Jim Hill jumped as if a tarantula had bit him.

" What's that? " he barked. " Yuh say he was ridin' a red horse? Big and tall and ice-eyed? "

" That's right," his informant replied wonderingly.

Jim Hill turned and bent his black glare on the younger Harlow.

" Yeah, you picked up a black diamond, all right," he rasped. " Yuh ganglin', no-brained splinter! Do yuh know who that was? "

" I don't know, and I don't give a damn! " bawled Wesley. " All I know is when I meet the blankety-blank-blank again I'll——"

" *Die!* " Jim cut in. " Yuh'd have about as much chance shadin' that sidewinder as a jackrabbit would have in a hounddawg's mouth. The next time yuh see that hellion *see his back!* Ride a red horse, eh? That hellion was Tom Carson, the hellion I been tellin' yuh about."

Wesley Harlow stopped swearing and stared at his brother open-mouthed.

" Tom Carson from Tombstone? Wyatt Earp's sidekick? "

" Uh-huh, now yuh know what yuh was up against? "

" Yeah, and I feel better'n I did," young Harlow returned. " They say he's got a faster gun hand than even Buckskin Frank Leslie had."

He added with vicious emphasis:

" And I'm takin' yore advice, Jim. The next time I'll see his back fust."

" See that yuh do," grunted Hill, " or he's liable to be the last thing yuh see this side of hell."

" Say, who is this jigger anyhow? " asked a squint-eyed cowboy who was new to Texas.

" He's the smartest and saltiest frontier doctor in Arizona," Hill replied slowly. " And he's plumb pizen with a gun."

" But," he added grimly, " I've a notion he's liable to git his come-uppance this time, if he tangles his twine with ourn. Yuh say he rode off with the Tree L chuck wagon? Yeah? Well, he's liable to be at their camp t'night. Hmmm! Mebbe this'll work out better'n expected. Is everythin' set up in that canyon, Barnes? Okay. They're shore to bed the herd there—all the drives headin' this way for Martin do. And I reckon it's about time we was ridin'. Getting past midnight. Let's go! "

At the Tree L camp all was quiet. Midnight came. The great clock in the sky wheeled westward. The cattle were resting easy. The drowsy night hawks found little to do. There was an occasional flicker of lightning in the west, and the intermittent mutter of thunder grew somewhat louder. Loud enough to be heard above the monotonous low rumble of the water tumbling down the end of the bench. Loud enough for Tom Carson's keen ears to catch the sound.

It was toward the dead hour before the dawn that Carson sat up in his blankets as a deeper mutter rolled up the overcast sky. He glanced keenly at the ragged veil of clouds, through the rents in which an occasional star peeped inquiringly.

" Looks like we might have a mite of rain after all," he told himself.

He glanced toward the western cliff wall, where he knew Rojo was holed up comfortably. His gaze swung back to the broken lip of the bench at the crest of the slope, where, back of the rimrock that walled it in, the deep and swift water worried along.

Over the lip of the rimrock had flashed a sudden tiny glow of light.

Carson was puzzled. " That darn thunder-storm isn't that far up in the sky," he muttered. " Must have been the reflection of a flash from a mica outcropping."

He continued to gaze at the dark lip lifting against the darker loom of the cliffs beyond the bench; but the flicker of light was not repeated. He yawned, prepared to settle down into his blanket once more. Then he shot to his feet as if propelled by a giant spring, instinctively snatching up his removed gun belts as he did so.

From the lip of the rimrock had burst a blinding glare of yellowish flame. Hard on the dazzling flash came a thudding boom.

As Carson stared in amazement, he was conscious that the crackling explosion was being echoed by a rumbling roar that swelled to a terrific tumult of sound. He blinked his eyes to clear them of the glare that had blinded him for the moment. As his vision reaccustomed itself to the dark that had rushed down almost instantly, he saw the pale vision that accompanied the thundering roar.

Down the rocky slope rushed an emerald wall topped by a froth of ghostly white, rolling boulders before it, engulfing them a moment later, racing at appalling speed toward the canyon floor.

Carson's voice pealed out in a yell that pierced the rushing thunder:

" Come out of it! Across to the westcliff. The dam's busted! "

Dazed, bewildered, the sleep-sodden cowboys were tumbling

out of their blankets, shouting dismay and apprehension. Under Carson's bellowed urging, they reeled and stumbled across the canyon.

Before they were halfway to the west wall, the flood was upon them, sweeping them off their feet, rolling them over and over in waist deep water as the diverted stream came roaring down the slope.

The bawling of the terrified cattle added to the tumult. The battering of their hoofs on the hard ground sounded above the bellow of the surging waters. Half swimmimg, half wading, they were swept to the mouth of the canyon, where the torrent swiftly spread over the prairie and shallowed.

Bawling and wailing, horns clashing, hoofs beating a drumroll of sound, the herd fled in mad stampede, the night hawks racing before them.

From beyond the canyon mouth came a wild yelling, and the crack of guns. Lead whined into the canyon, patting against the rocks, ricocheting with shrill screams.

One of the wading, wallowing cowboys let out a queer choking grunt, and vanished under the swirling water. Another cursed with pain and pawed at his blood streaming arm.

Tom Carson, sinewy legs wide apart, leaning back against the force of the water that coiled about his thighs, slid his guns from their holsters and sent a stream of hissing lead toward the flashes seen beyond the canyon mouth.

A derisive yell answered the shots, then the beat of fast hoofs driving after the fleeing herd. A few moments later, three distinctly spaced shots sounded in the distance.

At the base of the western cliffs, beyond the swirl and eddy of the diverted waters, the Tree L punchers huddled together, soaked to the skin, bruised, battered and seething with rage.

" Ev'body accounted for? " asked Old Man Sanderson, wringing the water from his beard.

" Curly Evans got it," replied a young waddie. " I saw him go down. He was drowned, even if the slug didn't do for him. Reckon everybody else is here except the night hawks, and they was in front of the stampede. Mebbe they made it in the clear."

" Mebbe," agreed Sanderson in a voice that carried no conviction to his hearers. Tom Carson, recalling those three ominously spaced shots, felt not the slightest doubt that the three night hawks would not be seen again as living men.

" But what the hell happened, anyhow? " somebody demanded. " How come the crik to be down here in the canyon? "

A moment of silence followed, then Carson spoke in his deep, musical voice.

" They dynamited the rimrock up there," he explained to his listeners. " Must have had it planted and all ready, figgering the herd would be bedded down here. One of them slipped up there and lit the fuse. The rest of the outfit were waiting outside the canyon for the herd to stampede out."

Old Man Sanderson swore viciously.

" It was the Harlows," he declared. " Nobody else woulda been smart enough to figger that out. Well, they got away with the herd, and cashed in four good men, the chances are."

His hands muttered downcast agreement. Heads were lifted as Carson spoke again.

" They haven't got away with it yet," he said. " That herd will travel slow after a hard day yesterday and a short rest. They'll run their legs off before those wideloopers can get them under control, and will be plumb blowed. We can catch up with them if we look sharp."

" By God, son, its' wuth tryin'! " declared Sanderson. " What's the fust move? "

" Round up the horses—they won't have strayed far," Carson instantly replied. " It'll be daylight in another hour and we can get started. Abe," he told the cook, " yore wagon is still on its wheels. See if yuh can get a fire started and some steaming coffee ready. That'll help after this wetting."

" We're gonna stay wet," a cowboy remarked in disgusted tones. " Now its' beginnin' to rain."

"Best thing that could happen," Carson assured him cheerfully. "Now they can't keep from leaving a trail for us to foller, no matter where they go. Up and at it, now—round up the horses and get the rigs on them. Lucky we put our saddles in the coonie last night."

The Tree L hands hastened to obey. Nobody seemed to think it worthy of remark that this latest addition to the outfit had usurped all the authority in sight. Even Old Man Sanderson himself, and Clate Gray, his foreman, didn't question Carson's orders, but got busy with the rest.

The dawn broke grey and misty with big drops falling steadily. But Carson, with a glance at the sky, delivered his opinion that the rain would stop shortly after the sun came up. The hands began to troop in with the horses. They were bedraggled and nervous, except Rojo, who had not moved from where he had holed up close to the cliff, and who regarded the unwonted activity with a mildly curious eye.

Dishonest Abe had managed to get a fire going and soon was dishing out welcome cups of hot coffee.

The body of Curly Evans had been found and lay decently covered with a blanket at the base of the cliffs. A little later, men who had gone to look for them brought in the bodies of the three night hawks, all of whom had been shot to death. With muttered oaths of vengeance they placed them beside that of Curly Evans.

As soon as the light had strengthened a bit, the Tree L punchers saddled up and took the trail of the widelooped herd.

Tom Carson rode in the lead, his steady grey eyes missing no detail of the landscape.

On the wet ground the trail left by the fleeing cattle was easy to follow. Not so easy, however, when a few miles further on, it veered more to the west and entered the mountainous terrain. Here the soil was stony and hard and had been little affected by the rain that was already letting up.

But Carson's keen eyes noted broken twigs, bent grass blades and overturned stones the others would have passed unnoticed.

"We're gaining on the hellions," he told Sanderson, several hours later.

The trail veered directly south once more and entered a vast hollow between two high and steep slopes. Both slopes and the floor of the narrow valley were densely grown with manzanita and other chaparral.

The sun was shining brightly now and it was hot and still in the brush grown depths. The trail, evidently a track that had been used more than once before, wound and tortured through the bristle of thicket. It was so narrow that the herd had left plenty of evidence of its passing in the nature of broken branches and scuffed stems.

On and on the trail wound. Only two men could ride abreast, now. Carson and Sanderson took the lead, the others crowding close behind.

The concentration furrow was deep between Carson's black brows as the sides of the hollow drew closer together and the growth, if anything, increased in density. It was a sure sign that the Tombstone doctor was doing some hard thinking.

"Easy," he cautioned Sanderson. "We don't want to run inter a drygulching. This is a plumb perfect section for one. We can't be over far behind the hellions now. Keep yore ears open for bellering. Those steers had oughta be getting mighty tired by now and begin talking about it."

Closer and closer drew the bristling slopes. The depths of the gorge were gloomy and there was a deathly stillness in which the sounds of their passage rang loud on the ear.

Suddenly Carson held up his hand, reining Rojo in sharply at the same moment.

"Listen," he said, "wasn't that a steer bawled?"

The sound came again, thin with distance, the querulous protest of weary, hungry and disgusted cattle. Carson's hand tightened on the bridle.

Then suddenly he eased off again, leaned forward in his hull and peered intently at the ribbon of sky ahead. The clean blue was fouled with a murky haze that rose from the growth.

Carson sniffed sharply. An acrid tang stung his nostrils. " Smoke! " he exclaimed. " Wood smoke! "

" Mebbe they've stopped to cook dinner," a young puncher hazarded.

" Cook dinner, hell! " Carson barked. " They've stopped to cook *us*, or I'm a heap mistook. Look at that smoke boil up. They've fired the brush to block us."

As a chorus of oaths arose from his followers, he whirled in his sadlle to stare back the way they had come. His face set in black lines. His eyes were icily cold.

" And they've fired it back of us, too," he said, gesturing toward the smoke that was falling up against the northern sky. " Gents, we're trapped! "

Chapter 9

An excited chorus arose as the Tree L punchers realized the full truth of Carson's statement. Bronzed faces lost their colour, eyes stared wildly. For a moment there was near panic.

"Hold it!" Carson's cool voice cut at them. "Hold it, we aren't done in yet."

The words had a steadying effect.

Carson eyed the slope on the left. It was fairly gradual, less brush grown than that on the right, which was rugged and precipitous and strewn with loose boulders.

"We can get up there to the left, mebbe, before the fire cuts us off," exclaimed Sanderson.

His men were already turning their horses to the left when Carson blared a warning.

"Not that way! That's the way the hellions will figger us to take. Ride up that sag and we'll be mowed down like jack rabbits at a barbecue."

"But good gosh, Carson, we can't ride up that sag, to the right!" wailed Clate Gray, the foreman. A chorus of dismayed agreement echoed his words.

"We've got to, and got to do it fast," Carson replied grimly. "That is unless yuh figger to be able to stand as much heat as yuh'll hafta in the hereafter. If we stay here, we'll be roasted like pigs in a barbecue. The fire is coming at us from both directions, and it's eating its way up the slopes, too. Look how those smoke clouds are widening out. Let's go!"

Cursing and muttering, the Tree L punchers sent their nervous horses at the sag. Staggering, scrambling, floundering over boulders, crashing through thorny growth that tore the clothes and scratched the faces of their riders and impeded their progress, they snorted up the slope that grew steeper and steeper. Before they were halfway to the rimrock, the cowboys were forced to dismount and toil on foot, dragging the frantic animals along.

And ever closer those thickening clouds of smoke. The air was hot, pungent with the smell of burning wood and scorching foliage, murky with flying ash. The sun overhead was obscured by a yellowish haze through which it glared like a jaundiced eye.

Tom Carson did not lead the van now. With Lafe Sanderson he brought up the rear, herding the stragglers ahead of him, urging the weaker to greater efforts.

Half way up the slope the retarding growth thinned somewhat and they slipped and slid over naked rock that bruised hands and knees and sapped their remaining strength.

Something yelled through the air over their heads, smacked against a stone and whined off at a tangent. Above the ominous crackling of the burning brush sounded a distant but sharper crack.

Tom Carson wheeled in his tracks, sliding his Winchester from the saddle boot as again came that lethal whine overhead. Motionless, alert, he stood outlined against the background of naked rock, with death spitting at him from the opposite slope and roaring toward him through the blazing brush. His eyes never left the distant crest of the sag on the far side of the hollow. His cocked rifle was gripped in his sinewy hands.

Once more a slug screeched past, so close that its deadly breath fanned his face.

But this time Carson had seen the tiny spiral of whitish smoke that marked the spot where the hidden drygulcher was holed up.

The rifle leaped to his shoulder. The stock cuddled against his cheek. His grey eyes glanced along the sights a second before he gave trigger.

A puff of smoke from the black muzzle. Another and another. With each shot Carson shifted the rifle barrel a fraction, raking the bush from whence had come that tell-tale whirl of smoke.

Suddenly the bush was violently agitated. Something dark pitched from it, rolled down the slope a little ways and was still.

Carson stood watchful and alert, his eyes glued to the brush fringed rimrock.

But no more bullets whined from the grey-green bristle. The slope remained devoid of sound or motion, hazily seen now through the swirling smoke clouds.

Carson lowered his rifle.

" That's one we won't hafta worry about," he told Lafe Sanderson, who had crouched as close to the ground as he could while the grim duel was in progress. " That'll be the jigger they had hang back to keep a watch on the trail behind and to signal the rest of the bunch when they had us where they wanted us. A salty outfit, all right. Don't stop at anything, and don't miss a trick. Let's go, that fire's almighty close."

The rest of the cowboys had plunged on and were now some distance further up the slope. Carson and Sanderson toiled to overtake them. The fire was roaring toward them from both directions. Ahead was more thick brush, tinder dry, which would offer fresh fuel for the flames.

" It's burnin' faster up in front," muttered Sanderson, squinting through the smoke with puckered eyes. " Son, it's gonna cut us off if we don't shake a leg. I believe the boys are gonna make it, but it's gonna be touch and go for you and me."

Carson nodded, saving his breath to climb the faster. The air was almost too hot to breathe, choked with smoke and flying ash. Ahead was a red glimmer that had almost closed the narrow gap that led to safety.

Another frantic hundred yards, and a gasping exclamation of despair from Lafe Sanderson.

There was no longer a dark opening between the two racing walls of flame. In front, behind and on both sides was a seething inferno.

" I'm done for! " gasped Sanderson. " We can't make it! "

" Keep goin'! " Carson barked at him. " There's just

G

a thin sheet of fire in front so far. We can dive through it. The rimrock is close."

" D-done for! " mumbled the old man, and pitched forward on his face.

Tom Carson whirled, strode back down the slope, picked up the limp form and swung it over his shoulder. He gripped the bridle of Sanderson's snorting horse with his free hand, turned and surged forward.

" Trail, Rojo! You can make it, feller! " he called to the great roan who scraped and floundered over the stones by his side.

Directly ahead was the wavering line of flame. Carson took a deep breath, ducked his head and plunged straight into it. The heat leaped at him like a living thing, sapping his strength, seeming to dry the blood in his veins. He felt the sear of the flames on his exposed hands, heard Sanderson's horse scream with pain. He reeled, staggered, almost fell, borne down by the heavy burden of the unconscious rancher. His head swam, red flashes stormed before his tightly closed eyes. His legs were turning to water and buckling beneath him.

His groping hand encountered something rough and crisp. Although he could not see through the welter of flame and smoke and swirling cinders, he knew it to be Rojo's tail.

" Trail feller! " he called hoarsely and grimly held on.

He heard Rojo snort explosively, felt him surge forward. He was almost dragged off his feet, but he managed to keep his balance and automatically work legs that did not seem to belong to him.

A final searing blast, a gush of choking smoke acrid with the steamed juice of scorched leaves, and then a brush of air, comparatively cool, that fanned his face. He opened his eyes that he had held tightly shut while in the thickest of the fire, and saw, directly ahead, a bare slope leading up to the growth free rimrock a hundred feet farther on.

From the rimrock, where the Tree L hands were clustered,

peering despairingly through the smoke, came a roar of voices. Men plunged down the slope to relieve Slade of his burden, and to help drag the almost spent horses to safety. Others supported Carson, who quickly regained strength as he gulped in great draughts of blessed air.

On the rimrock, which was comparatively free from smoke, Sanderson also quickly revived. He got to his feet, somewhat shakily, and regarded Carson.

" Son," he said heavily, " yuh can't thank a feller right for what you just done, so I ain't even goin' to try. Did yuh get burned much? "

" Oh, just a mite of a patch here and there," replied Carson, who was surveying the further slope, which was much less steep than the one they had just surmounted. It led to the floor of the narrow valley that extended due south for as far as the eye could reach. It looked encouraging.

" And old Rojo didn't lose more'n a mite of hair," he added with a chuckle. " Reckon we all came out of it sorta lucky."

" I wouldn't call it luck," grunted Clate Gray. " I'd call it damn smart thinkin' on yore part that saved us. If it hadn't been for you, the lot of us would be buzzard bait by now."

The Tree L punchers nodded emphatic assent.

" Well," remarked Sanderson, " I figger we can make it down that sag to the bottom, and then we'd oughta be able to get back to the spread."

But when they reached the valley floor, the slope being negotiated with little difficulty, Tom Carson turned Rojo's head south.

" Where *you* goin'? " demanded Sanderson. " The spread is back the other way."

" After that herd," Carson told him grimly. " I figger this valley is a straight shoot for the Line. Those hellions will run the herd across and dispose of it below the Border. I've a notion it'll be possible to get ahead of them and mebbe have a little surprise ready for them down in manana land when they get there."

" You figger to go it alone? " demanded Sanderson.

" Would sorta help to have two or three dependable gents along," Carson admitted.

Old Lafe Sanderson turned his horse's head.

" Them's my beefs what's been stole," he said, " and I reckon I don't aim to send anybody to bring 'em back so long as I'm able to fork a hull."

Clate Gray also turned south. The rest of the Tree L hands followed suit.

But Carson shook his head.

" One more man along with you and Clate will be enough," he told Sanderson. " This is gonna take some outsmartin', and too big a crowd is liable to smear the deal."

" That's sense," agreed old Lafe. He beckoned a rangy cowboy with sunken cheeks and deep-set eyes.

" You come along, Carter," he directed. " Yuh're about the best shot in the outfit, and I reckon a ac'rate gunhand is liable to be in order on this trip."

Chapter 10

As Carson had anticipated, the valley led straight to the Border, which they crossed. Taking a southward slanting course to the east, just as night was falling they struck a well travelled trail.

" I know something of this section down here," Carson told the others. " A few miles farther on along this track is a town, and I've a mighty strong hunch that it is a pueblo that's used as a sorta clearing station for wet beefs. Yeah, I figger it's there those hellions will make connection with a buyer. We'll get there fust and see what's what."

Carson was right as to his bearings. Full dark had fallen when they saw ahead the twinkling lights of a town set in the shadow of a hill.

" But won't it attract attention, four jiggers ridin' in like this? " Sanderson suggested.

" Not if we play our cards right," Carson returned. " This is a lively little pueblo and lots of Border riding gents drop along here from time to time. We'll make out to be a bunch in on a bust. Gents don't always mention down this-a-way just where they came from last, and it isn't the usual thing for anybody to ask questions. Folks here take yuh as yuh come, and yuh're okay till yuh prove otherwise. These folks down this side of the Line are sociable and good natured so long as yuh don't kick over the traces and rub 'em the wrong way. They can be plenty salty if necessary, but they aren't out on the prod against strangers just because they are strangers."

As Carson predicted, the town proved lively. There was a lighted plaza, and a number of cantinas. Carson entered one, while the others waited outside, and inquired as to the whereabouts of a reliable stable in which their horses could

be cared for.   The courteous proprietor directed him to one
and after giving the stable keeper a quick oneover, Carson
decided that the cayuses would be safe in his care.   This
chore off their hands, they returned to the cantina and
proceeded to simulate a carefree bunch out for diversion.

Carson noted that at the bar and throughout the room
was a fair sprinkling of Texans and others from north of the
Line.   Some had the appearance of roving cowboys who
had drifted down this way, while others, Carson decided
were gents whose antecedents might not bear investigation;
their presence, neither, for that matter, and their futures
questionable.

A good orchestra played plaintive Mexican airs and there
were plenty of sloe-eyed señoritas in evidence on the dance
floor.

Chucka-luck games were in progress, three-card monte,
and poker.   There was a faro bank doing a rousing business
and several roulette wheels spinning merrily.   The careless
garb of riders from north of the River mingled with the more
colourful costume of Mexican vaqueros.

Carson danced with several of the attractive, dark-haired
girls.   Old Man Sanderson tried his hand at chuck-a-luck.
Clate Gray and Carter gave the roulette wheels a whirl.
Together they had several drinks at the bar.

" We're getting away with it, all right," Carson told his
companions.   " At fust we got some pretty sharp looks, but
now nobody's paying any attention to us.   We'll take in
a couple more places, and if anybody is really keeping an eye
on us, they'll decide we're nothing but what we look to be."

They visited several more cantinas.   Finally, not long
before midnight, Carson told the others—

" Now we'll get down to business.   Across the street is
our next stop."

He led the way to a cantina somewhat smaller than the others
they   had   visited.   A   pleasant   faced,   comfortably   fleshy
Mexican standing at the far end of the bar glanced up at
their entrance, stared, and hurried forward to meet them.

" El Curador! " he greeted Carson in low tones. " Welcome, Señor Medico! "

" Howdy, Miguel? " Carson responded. " Remember me from Tombstone, eh? How's everything by you? Meet my amigos. We sorta hanker to put on the nosebag. Haven't s'rounded any chuck for so long our tapeworms are figgering on moving to new quarters."

The cantina proprietor led the way to a table and summoned a waiter. Sanderson and his hands seated themselves. While the food was being prepared, Carson joined Miguel at the end of the bar and engaged him in conversation.

" Amigo, who in this section buys beefs that happen to wander down across the River and get lost? " he asked.

The proprietor hesitated, glanced furtively over his shoulder to see if anyone was within hearing distance.

" I'm not on the prod against the buyer, no matter who he is," Carson hastened to reassure him. " I have no right to interfere with anybody down here south of the Border, but I am sorta int'rested in a herd that might stray somewhere in this direction about tonight some time. Can't tell just exactly where they'll cross, but figger somebody here will know about it."

Miguel glanced around once before replying.

" Felipe Garcia usually buys the cattle that—er—stray across the Line," he said in low tones. " Si, it is usually known here in the pueblo when cattle drift this way. A messenger is sent from here to Garcia's hacienda, which is some forty miles to the south. The messenger arranges a meeting point for Garcia's agent and those who—stray with the cattle."

" I see," Carson nodded. " I wonder, Miguel, if there'd be any chance of that messenger being stopped, and somebody taking his place? "

Miguel raised his eyes to meet Carson's steady gaze.

" A suggestion by El Curador is an order," he murmured. " Wait here, Señor."

He sauntered casually across the room to where a group

was gathered around a monte table. After speaking with several of the group in an off-hand manner, he strolled back to the end of the bar. A few minutes later a man left the group, paused at the bar, close to where Miguel stood, and ordered a drink. He had a lean dark face, a hawk nose and high cheek bones. His lank black hair was cut in a bang across his forehead.

A single glance told Carson that he was a pure-blood Yaqui Indian.

"This is Esteban," Miguel said in low tones. "He will stop the messenger before he reaches Garcia, and will return as the one Garcia sends to arrange the meeting."

Carson spoke in perfect Spanish.

"No killing, Estaban. No real harm must come to the messenger. He'll just he a hired hand working for Garcia and making what he figures is an honest living."

The Yaqui nodded his understanding.

"Come to me when you return, and I will tell you what word to bear to those who await the messenger," Miguel added.

Again Estaban inclined his head the merest fraction. He finished his drink and sauntered out.

"Señor, it will be simple," said Miguel. "Garcia always designates the point of rendezvous. Nor is the messenger who goes to Garcia and he who bears the word to those who wait always the same. But at the place of meeting, Señor, I fear for you. Those who will wait the word are 'muy malo hombres'."

Carson was willing to agree that the Harlows and their bunch were indeed "very bad men," but he merely nodded his appreciation of Miguel's well meant warning.

"We'll want a place where we can pound our ears tonight and keep out of sight tomorrow," he told the cantina owner.

"Si, it is simple," Miguel replied. That I will arrange."

Carson and his companions enjoyed an ample meal. Meanwhile, Miguel arranged to transfer their horses to his own stable. Then he conducted them to a couple of quiet rooms over the cantina.

" It's like this," Carson explained to the others. " Estaban will intercept the messenger on his way to Garcia. It's an open secret hereabouts that wet cattle are bought here and then driven south, where there is a ready market for them in which the local purchaser can just about double his money. Garcia is evidently the big buyer in this section. He's got plenty of savvy and keeps in the clear. He has men on the lookout here for herds that are being driven across. These men contact the rustlers and arrange for them to meet with Garcia's representative and turn the beefs over to him. My amigo Miguel always knows what's going on. I happen to know he doesn't have anything to do with this kind of a business, and so long as we don't make trouble for somebody on this side of the Line he's willing to lend me a hand."

" Yuh think he'll take a chance on getting the Harlows on the prod against him? " Sanderson asked.

" Oh, Miguel is a good egg, and he knows the Harlows aren't out to do any good for anybody down here," Carson equivocated. He did not see fit to mention that he had once saved Miguel's life.

" But how will Estaban know who the messenger is? " Clate Gray asked.

Carson shrugged his broad shoulders.

" Trust a Yaqui to know everything that's going on," he replied. " For all we know, Estaban may be the messenger himself. Anyhow, he takes orders from Miguel, and Miguel evidently figgers he knows what he's about. All we got to do is sit tight, and be ready to act pronto when the time comes. Now I've a notion we could do with a mite of shuteye. We didn't get over much last night, and it's been a busy day."

They spent the following day in the rooms. Miguel himself brought them food.

The lovely blue dusk was sifting down from the hills and the sky was aflame with gold and scarlet when he again appeared, after supper. He carefully closed and locked the door behind him, glanced at the windows to make sure the shutters were tightly closed.

"It is done, Señor," he told Carson. "Tonight the cattle came to the mouth of Embrujada Valley, whence a trail leads to Garcia's hacienda. Those who bring the cattle were told by Estaban that Garcia's agent meets with them there."

"How do we get to the valley?" Carson asked.

"Trouble not your mind about that," the cantina owner replied. "I, Miguel, will guide you. Perhaps I may even be some small assistance when the moment comes."

"No sense in you taking chances of getting mixed up in the shindig when it comes off," Carson objected.

Miguel smiled, and shrugged his shoulders with Latin expressiveness.

"And there was not the sense, perhaps, in El Curador once mixing himself in—what you call it—the smallpox in Miguel's behalf; but Miguel does not forget," he replied. "In the hour, Señor, it will be dark. Prepare you to ride."

Chapter 11

EMRUJADA VALLEY lay like a gaping mouth in the craggy face of the hills. Through it flowed a trail, a trail that birthed in the mountains of Arizona. Southward the trail flowed, to lose itself among the purple mountains of Mexico.

A full moon was rising from behind the hills to the east, but the valley was still black with shadow.

From the dark north came a sound, a sound that steadily grew in volume until it identified itself as the slow beat of many hoofs. A vast moving shadow appeared in the mouth of the valley. It moved forward, ever more slowly, and came to a halt.

Other shadows detached themselves from the main body, moved still further ahead. Gruff voices sounded. The ghostly glimmer of the moonlight strengthened and the moving shadows were revealed as horsemen looming gigantic in the dusk.

Near the black eastern wall of the valley a tiny light flickered. There was a crackling roar and a soaring burst of flame as oil soaked brush caught fire from Miguel's match and burned fiercely, making the scene as bright as day.

The Harlow bunch jerked their horses to a halt and sat staring in slack-jawed bewilderment at the grim figures confronting them, rifles at the ready.

Tom Carson's voice rang out, edged with steel—

" Elevate! Yuh're covered! "

" Caught settin' ", utterly astounded at this sudden appearance of the men they thought fifty miles distant, if they thought of them at all, the wideloopers hesitated, seemed about to obey.

It was Wesley Harlow who suddenly let out a scream of rage.

" It's him, damn him! " he howled, and went for his guns.

A split second later he thudded to the earth, Carson's bullet laced through his heart.

The hills rocked and trembled to the roar of gunfire as the outlaws, galvanized by Wesley's reckless move, went into action.

Sanderson, Gray and Carter, the lanky cowboy, were firing as fast as they could pull trigger. Two saddles were emptied at their first volley. Gray reeled as a bullet grazed his forehead, but he steadied himself and downed the man who had shot him.

The three remaining outlaws whirled their horses to flee. Again the rifles cracked, and a riderless horse plunged forward and was entangled in the welter of terrified, milling cattle.

The other wideloopers, bending low in the saddle, veered to the right, flashed through the stragglers and thundered north along the trail.

Tom flung up his rifle, took quick aim and fired. He saw one of the fleeing horsemen wince as the bullet came close. Again he squeezed the trigger, and heard the hammer click sharply on an empty shell.

With a muttered oath, he stuffed fresh cartridges into the magazine. Then he ran to where Rojo stood, sheathed the Winchester and flung himself into the saddle.

" Shove the herd nawth," he shouted to his companions. " That was Sime Harlow and Jim Hill that got away, or I'm a heap mistook. Trail, Rojo! "

The trail was completely blocked by the milling herd and Rojo was forced to pick his way carefully over the broken ground to the left. Minutes passed before his irons again thudded on the level surface.

Carson settled himself in the saddle.

" Get goin', jughead! " he called. " That hellion's got a start, now. Yuh got yore work cut out for yuh."

Rojo snorted, slugged his head above the bit and literally poured his long body over the ground, his hoofs beating a drumroll of sound.

Ten minutes later, peering ahead through the strengthening

moonlight, Carson saw a rider outlined on the crest of a distant rise and going like the wind.

Faster and faster sped the great red horse. His eyes rolled, his nostrils flared, he snorted with the excitement of the pursuit. Carson encouraged him with voice and hand, steadied him, swaying his body in perfect balance with the horse's efforts.

Another rise swelling ahead, and again the fleeing outlaws came into view, much closer this time. They vanished over the crest.

Carson sent Rojo surging up the long slope of the rise. He topped it, scudded down the opposite sag, crashed through a belt of thicket, veered around a jutting shoulder of rock. Carson's hand hauled back on the bridle with all his strength.

Not two hundred yards ahead, rifle stock cuddled against his cheek, Sime Harlow sat his motionless horse.

Carson flung himself sideways from the saddle as Rojo skated on legs braced like steel rods. The wind of a passing bullet fanned his face.

As he fell he gripped the stock of his Winchester. His one chance of life hinged on the rifle not sticking in the boot.

He struck the ground hard, the rifle gripped in his hands, rolled over and snapped a shot under Rojo's belly, knew he had missed. Harlow's answering bullet showered his face with dust. Blinking, half blinded, he fired again.

There was a sudden drumming of hoofs. Harlow was racing his horse toward the fallen Carson firing as he came. Bullets spatted the ground beside Carson, whined viciously past. One twitched at his sleeve like an urging hand. He took careful aim and squeezed the stock.

Harlow jolted in his saddle and Carson knew he had scored a hit. But the outlaw still came on.

Harlow wore a large brass belt buckle that gleamed in the moonlight. Steadying himself, Carson outlined his front sight squarely aganst the shifting gleam and pulled trigger.

He heard the bullet strike, saw Sime Harlow whirl from the saddle and lie writhing on the ground.

Carson got to his feet and cautiously approached the fallen outlaw, whose movements were growing feebler. Another moment and he knelt beside the dying man.

Sime Harlow glared up into his face with eyes of hellish hate.

" You win, damn yuh! " he gasped. " Why in hell did yuh hafta bust inter my game? "

Tom Carson slowly shook his head. He was fumbling at a cunningly concealed secret pocket in his broad leather belt. He held something before the dying outlaw's eyes. Something that glittered in the moonlight It was a silver shield—the feared and honoured badge of the federal marshals!

Sime Harlow gulped in his blood welling throat. He stared unbelievingly at the symbol of law and order.

"A United States Marshal! " he panted.

" Yes," Carson told him. " I didn't come to bust inter your game, Harlow. I come to get Jim Hill, but it looks like he's given me the slip again, thanks to you."

Sime Harlow strove to speak, but choked on the blood in his throat instead, and, choking, died. Carson stood up, staring into the shadowy north, into which Jim Hill had vanished.

South of the Line, Carson and his companions shook hands with Miguel.

" Come again, Señor Medico," the smiling Mexican urged. " El Curador, the friend of the lowly, is always welcome."

The recovered herd was shoved across the Border just as dawn was breaking, and headed north. A few miles farther on the trail forked, one branch flowing westward. Here Carson pulled Rojo to a halt.

" But ain'tcha ridin' back to the spread with us? " protested Sanderson. " I'd shore like to have yuh stay with me. Besides," he added significantly, " there's a big reward due on Sime Harlow, and I figger yuh're the feller to cash in on it."

But Tom smilingly shook his head.

" Never figgered any good ever came outa that kind of

money," he declined. "There's a feller somewhere ahead I'm sorta anxious to see, so I reckon I'll just be trailing my rope. Been nice to have known you fellers—we had a nice time together." He turned Rojo's head westward.

"Reckon we'd might as well head back for Tombstone," he told the horse. "I've a notion things have been happening since we left there."

Things *had* been happening in Tombstone during Carson's absence. The stage road between Tombstone and Bisbee circled the Mule Mountains to the westward, followed the level stretches of the San Pedro Valley through Charleston and Hereford and came into Bisbee from the south. The stage team was climbing a grade three miles beyond Hereford at eleven o'clock at night. The moon was sinking and cast a reddish glow over the lonely mountains. The night was still and the creak of harness leather and the jingle of chains sounded loudly. The driver, unaccompanied by a shotgun messenger, half drowsed on his seat. There were four passengers aboard, three inside and one sitting outside on the box. The grade was steep and the horses travelled at a walk. They shied as two masked men armed with shotgun and six-shooter stepped out of the mesquite.

The bandits rifled the pockets of the passengers and got $2500 from the Wells-Fargo express box. They worked in the business-like manner of old hands at the game, wished everybody a pleasant good night and vanished into the mesquite.

A Tombstone posse took the trail the following morning. Wyatt and Morgan Earp were members of the posse. Within a week, Frank Stillwell and Pete Spence, both members of Curly Bill Graham's gang and friends of the Clantons and McLowerys were arrested for the robbery by Wyatt and Morgan Earp. They were brought to Tombstone and released on bail.

The evidence against Stillwell and Spence was slight. They had stopped at a cobbler's shop in Bisbee, where Stillwell had a narrow pair of heels removed from his almost new boots and replaced with a broad pair. The suspicious cobbler reported the incident. The narrow heels from Stillwell's boots fitted tracks left at the scene of the robbery.

Stillwell and Spence had been suspected of other stage robberies, although nothing was ever proved against them.

The stagecoach passengers insisted that a third man stood back in the shadows with a levelled rifle during the course of the robbery.

" And I'm a plumb good notion who that third man was," Sheriff Behan declared grimly. " Every time a certain jigger vanishes out of this town for a spell, something like this happens. He's smart all right. Gettin' somethin' on him is like puttin' yore finger on a horse fly on a hot day. But he'll slip yet! "

Although Behan mentioned no names, folks knew that his suspicions were directed toward Tom Carson.

" Behan's loco," Wyatt Earp scoffed, and others were also of that opinion. But there were still others who pointed out that Carson was undoubtedly friendly with Doc Holliday, who himself was under suspicion of having taken part in the Benson stage robbery; and the matter of the hundred-dollar bill found in Carson's possession had never been cleared up to the satisfaction of many.

Much of Sheriff Behan's vindictive suspicion was doubtless based on the friendship that had developed between Carson and Wyatt Earp, the sheriff's hated political rival.

Carson learned of the Bisbee stage robbery when he arrived in Tombstone. It had occurred nearly three weeks before. He learned other things when he dropped into Doc Goodfellow's office for a professional chat.

" Things are shaping up hereabouts for a showdown," said Goodfellow. " Something's bustin' loose every day. John Ringo challenged Doc Holliday to a handkerchief duel down in front of Bob Hatch's saloon. Holliday was willing. They each had hold of one corner of a bandana and were reaching for their guns when Mayor Thomas jumped in between them and stopped the shindig before it got started. Ringo had just got through offering to shoot it out with Wyatt Earp in the middle of the street, at ten paces. Wyatt laughed at him and told him to go to bed and sleep it off. Then he tackled Holliday. Then Ringo held up a poker game over in Evilsizer's saloon in Galeyville. The players squawked to the sheriff and Deputy Bill Breakenridge brought Ringo in. The sheriff let him go, figuring bail was being arranged. The Earps had gotten the district attorney's permissiom to keep Ringo locked up without bail for twenty-four hours."

"Why did they want that done?" Carson asked.

" They wanted to get Curly Bill Graham," Goodfellow replied. " Curly Bill was supposed to have held up the stage at Robbers' Roost. The Earps had located him at Charleston and figured he'd be drunk on the loot. With Ringo out of the way, it would be easy. But when they got to Charleston, and started to cross the bridge across the San Pedro to town, there was John Ringo at the far end of the bridge with a rifle. The Earps didn't cross nacherly. They came back to town madder'n wet hens. Next morning the judge was just starting to give Johnny Behan merry blue blazin' hell for letting Ringo loose. In walks Ringo with Billy Breakenridge! He'd heard Behan was in for trouble and rode all night to get back in time. Funny how those outlaws look out for Johnny, isn't it?"

"Very funny," Carson returned grimly.

Doc Goodfellow chuckled, and stuffed tobacco into his pipe.

" This business of the Earps arresting Frank Stillwell and Pete Spence is liable to bring the showdown sooner," Goodfellow resumed. " They're both close friends of the Clantons and the McLowerys, who have sworn to kill the Earps and Doc Holliday. Between you and me, I figger the Earps have got more to be scairt of from Stillwell and Spence than they have from the others. A row is going to break between them and the Clantons and McLowerys sooner or later, but it will be a straight to the face shooting! Stillwell and Spence are the knife in-the-back kind, and they're vicious as a hydrophobia skunk with a sore tooth."

Carson nodded thoughtfully. He was something of the

H

same opinion. Stillwell and Spence were bad characters. Stillwell, he knew spent considerable time swallerforkin' around the Tombstone dance halls. He gambled a lot, drank moderately, and always had plenty of money—more than the livery stable he owned in Charleston could possibly earn. He was known as a quick-draw man and very accurate with a sixshooter. He was under thirty.

Pete Spence was at least forty and was supposed to be a gambler. He had a reputation as a killer in the Big Bend country of Texas and elsewhere.

"That ornery half-breed, Injun Charlie Cruz, has been sneaking around with Spence and Stillwell since they were turned loose on bail," Goodfellow observed. "He's pizen as a sidewinder and just as slithery. A fine bunch, Carson, a fine bunch!"

The ominous storm cloud that was gathering over Tombstone darkened rapidly. The feud betwen the Earps and the outlaws of Cochise county was becoming more bitter with each passing day. In Tombstone the Earps were supreme. Their following was large and influential. Wyatt and Virgil Earp had cleaned up Tombstone, had established a regime of law and order. The owlhoots whose stronghold was the Dragoons resented this change. They were powerful and well organized, perhaps the most powerful and boldest outfit of its kind the Southwest had ever known. They hated the Earps and all they represented with a bitter intensity.

The Clantons and McLowerys formed the spearhead of the organization. Curly Bill Graham, shrewd as he was deadly, kept in the background. Since the day, nearly two years before, that Marshal White was killed in a scuffle with Curly Bill while relieving the outlaw chief of his gun, and Wyatt Earp bent a sixshooter over Curly Bill's head, Curly Bill had given Tombstone a wide berth; but his bitterness against Wyatt Earp increased as time passed. This bitterness had not been lessened when Virgil Earp became Marshal to succeed White, for whose death Curly Bill was, to some extent, at least, responsible.

Curly Bill could not fail to see that because of the death of Marshal White, the Earps, with Virgil head of police activities in the town, and Wyatt holding an important Federal position, the Earps were on the road to become politically powerful. Curly Bill dreaded the day when Wyatt Earp would be elected sheriff to succeed Johnny Behan. He saw that the same law and order purge inflicted on Tombstone was in a fair way to spread to all of Cochise county. The only way to prevent such a catastrophe was to eliminate the Earps or break their power. Curly Bill plotted to achieve this result. The Clantons and McLowerys and their ilk were tools shaped to this end by the master workman.

All of which concerned Tom Carson. He liked and admired Wyatt Earp, and, despite his all too evident faults, he liked the saturnine Holliday, who had rugged, robust qualities that, in Carson's estimation, outweighed the negative ones.

Carson feared the outcome of the explosion that appeared inevitable. He felt that no matter what the immediate results of a clash between the two factions, it would ultimately mean the end of the Earps in Tombstone. Already a feeling was building up that Tombstone would be better off without Earp control. The affair of the Benson road had left them under a cloud of suspicion. Sheriff Behan, tricky, shrewd, a master at the intricate game of politics, was leaving no stone unturned in his efforts to minimize their influence in civic and county affairs. As a man, Johnny Behan was of small calibre, but as a politician he was formidable. His subtle manœuvres were more effective than the shoot-from-the-hip policies of the Earps, who scorned subterfuge and relied on direct methods

It was pot-valiant, blustering Ike Clanton who touched off the powder keg. Ike got drunk and had a run-in with Doc Holliday. Holliday, in a blazing rage, accused Clanton of lying about him to Wyatt Earp. He called Clanton everything available to a rich and colourful vocabulary of opprobrium, and dared Clanton to fight it out on the spot. Ike had left his rifle and Colt behind the bar at the Grand

Hotel, doubtless as a law abiding gesture that would tend to put him in the right, knowing that he could easily arm himself elsewhere should occasion arise. He backed down before Holliday's vicious challenge. Finally Marshal Virgil Earp threatened to put both men in jail if they didn't cool down. Clanton walked away. Holliday entered a saloon and it looked like the row was over for the time at least.

But Clanton continued to drink, and mouth threats against the Earps, and Holliday.

Tom Carson, whose status as a doctor gave him standing with both factions, sought Ike Clanton out and talked earnestly with him.

" I know you're a square shooter, Carson, even if yuh are a friend of the Earps," Clanton said. " Yuh saved my brother's life, and yuh've helped others of the boys; but nobody can talk to me like Holliday did and get away with it. I'm goin' to kill him."

" Go to bed, Ike, and yuh'll feel different about the whole thing in the morning," Carson urged.

But the next day, Ike Clanton was still on the warpath. He was armed with a Winchester and a sixgun. He swore he'd kill Doc Holliday or the first Earp who appeared on the street. Billy Clanton, Tom and Frank McLowery arrived in town and joined him.

Marshal Virgil Earp met Ike Clanton on Fourth Street. Clanton threw up his rifle threateningly. Virgil Earp grabbed the barrel and bent his sixgun over Clanton's head, knocking him sprawling.

Wyatt and Morgan Earp, who had observed the struggle, hurried to their brother's aid. They disarmed Clanton and took him to Justice Wallace.

By this time Wyatt Earp was in a black rage. He told Ike Clanton off proper and left the courtroom. In the street he met Tom McLowery. McLowery challenged Wyatt Earp to a fight then and there. Wyatt slapped McLowery's face, belted him over the head with the barrel of his Colt and knocked him bleeding into the gutter. McLowery had a gun, but did not attempt to use it. Wyatt Earp walked away and left him lying in the gutter, streaming blood and mouthing curses, but making no hostile move.

Tom Carson did not witness this incident, but a little later he met the Clantons, the McLowerys and Billy Claiborne walking together in a tight group. All were armed. They paused as Carson came up, and eyed him silently for a moment.

" Better go to yore office and stay there, Doc," Billy Claiborne advised. " We're out to get the Earps, and if you ain't lookin' for trouble yoreself, yuh'd better keep away from them."

"Reckon I can take care of any trouble that comes my way," Carson replied evenly.

" Yeah, I've heard yuh've made big talk in yore time, but yuh'd better keep outa my way," Claiborne answered. " I ain't Jim Hill, Carson, so don't try to shade me, or yuh'll be sorry."

" I'm not looking for trouble with yuh, Claiborne," Carson told him. " Fact is I don't figger yuh're capable of making any real trouble for anybody. I've a notion yuh don't over like the smell of powder smoke."

Claiborne grew fiery red under his tan. He glared at Carson, glanced down at the doctor's beltless waist.

" You get heeled the next time we meet, and see if I'm scairt of powder smoke! " he blustered.

Frank McLowery took Claiborne by the arm.

" Come along, Billy, and let the Doc alone," he urged. " We got business to 'tend to."

" And when yuh see the Earps, tell them we're waitin' for them," he flung at Carson as he started Claiborne down the street.

Carson walked thoughtfully to the Oriental. He found the Earps and Doc Holliday there, looking grave.

" Did yuh see anythin' of the Clantons? " Wyatt Earp asked.

" They're headed for the O. K. corral, and they're making big medicine," Carson told him.

Wyatt Earp tugged at his moustache. "There's goin' to be trouble," he predicted. "Come on, let's have a drink. Then we'll mosy outside for a breath of fresh air."

A little later, as they stood at the corner of Fourth and Allen streets, R. C. Coleman rushed up to them excitedly, pausing to catch his breath.

"I met the Clantons and McLowerys a little while ago, down by the O. K. corral," he said. "They're heeled, and talkin' fight. Yuh' better look out."

The Earps and Holliday glanced at each other. Wyatt's big jaw tightened.

"We've got to disarm those fellers and lock 'em up," he said. "Come on."

"Wait a minute for me," said Carson, "I'm going along."

"You keep outa this, son," Wyatt Earp said kindly. "It's our chore, and it may end up in trouble."

"I'm a deputy federal marshal the same as you," Carson told him in low tones. "It's as much my chore as yores. I'm going for my guns."

He turned and hurried back toward his office. Wyatt Earp gazed after him a moment, then turned to his companions.

"Come on," he repeated.

Sheriff Behan had hurried off to find the Clantons and McLowerys, whom he proposed to disarm. He found them standing in a vacant lot near the O. K. corral on Fremont Street with Billy Claiborne. The Clantons and McLowerys and Claiborne refused to be disarmed. Ike Clanton and Tom McLowery claimed to be unarmed. But Billy Clanton's and Frank McLowery's horses stood within arm's reach, and hanging from the pommel of each saddle was a Winchester rifle.

His mission a failure, Sheriff Behan hurried back up the street to find the Earps. He met them and Doc Holliday coming along the west side of Fremont Street, their faces grimly set, their eyes fixed on the little group in the vacant lot alongside the corner building.

Doc Holliday was, as usual, dressed in impeccable taste. Under his light grey overcoat he carried a sawed-off shot-gun strapped to his shoulder. He was also armed with a sixgun. The Earps wore black clothes and were armed with sixshooters.

Sheriff Behan met them. He gabbled protests, waved his hands excitedly. Wyatt Earp brushed him aside as if he were a fly. With businesslike strides, the grim four drew near the group in the vacant lot. Sheriff Behan followed, still protesting; but at the front door of Fly's photo gallery, a little distance away, he paused where he could seek safety if necessary.

Tom Carson secured his guns and buckled them on. His face was bleak, his eyes coldly grey, for he knew the moment he had dreaded was at hand. The showdown was coming. He knew, also, that he could do nothing to prevent it. Hitching his cartridge belts a little higher about his lean waist, he left his office and walked swiftly toward the corral. As he turned the corner of Fourth Street, the Earps were perhaps a hundred paces in front of him.

Carson saw the Clantons and McLowerys and Billy Claiborne waiting in the vacant lot. He also saw something else.

On the far side of Fremont Street, which here was a wide avenue, he saw two men walking furtively some twenty paces behind the Earps, who had eyes only for the group on the vacant lot. Carson recognized Frank Stillwell and Pete Spence. Instantly he diagonalled across the street to the east side of Fremont, lengthened his stride and, walking silently, closed in on Stillwell and Spence.

The Earps halted directly in front of the Clantons and McLowerys, and within arm's length of them. Stillwell and Spence also halted. They were perhaps ten paces behind the Earps, and with the width of the street between them. Carson saw their hands steal stealthily down. He took a long stride and touched Stillwell on the shoulder.

" Yuh'll not shoot Wyatt Earp in the back today, Stillwell," he said quietly.

Stillwell whirled. His face convulsed with fury. His hand gripped his gun but lingered there.

Carson hit him with his left hand. His slim, steely fist connected squarely with the point of Stillwell's chin. Stillwell lifted off the ground, shot through the air and crashed to the street to lie soddenly limp, blood flowing from his nose and mouth.

Spence also reached for his gun, but before he could clear leather, the muzzle of Carson's right-hand Colt jabbed hard against his belly.

" Turn around," Carson told him.

Spence, his face whitening before the blazing glare of Carson's grey eyes, obeyed, dropping his hand to his side. Carson plucked his gun from its holster and stuck it in his own belt.

But Pete Spence did not seem to even notice. He was staring with bulging eyes at the groups in the vacant lot across the street.

" God! " he gasped, " the ball's opened!"

Carson, gazing over Spence's shoulder, saw the hands of Billy Clanton and Frank McLowery flash down and up. He also saw the guns of Wyatt and Morgan Earp blaze fire.

Billy Clanton fell against the wall of the building behind him. He slid to the ground on his back. He drew himself up on one knee, gripped his gun in both hands and continued to fight.

Frank McLowery screamed as Wyatt Earp's slug took him in the belly. He clapped his left hand to the wound and staggered blindly about for a moment.

Tom McLowery sprang behind his brother's horse to get his rifle, but Wyatt Earp, with the utmost coolness, creased the horse's withers with a bullet and it plunged away. McLowery grabbed for the rifle in the boot and missed it. McLowery shot at Wyatt with a sixgun, but at that instant Doc Holliday threw open his overcoat, seized the sawed-off shotgun that hung in its loop to his right shoulder and fired both barrels at Tom McLowery.

The heavy double charges of buckshot lifted McLowery clean off his feet and crashed him to the earth; but with unbelievable tenacity of life he got to his feet again, reeled around the corner toward Third Street, and fell lifeless.

Ike Clanton, gibbering with terror, ran forward and frantically gripped Wyatt Earp by the arm. Wyatt hurled him off and Ike turned and ran into the open door of Fly's photo gallery. Billy Claiborne fired three shots at Virgil Earp, all of which missed, darted across the street and vanished into the photo gallery in the wake of Ike Clanton.

Carson saw this. He ran his eye along the wall of the gallery. There was a side window opening onto the vacant lot where the fight was in progress. The setting was perfect for a murderous drygulching. Carson bounded across the street and darted through the open door of the gallery. He raced to the back room, guns out and ready.

Ike Clanton and Billy Claiborne were crouched by the side window, guns raised. They whirled as Carson entered. Claiborne, with a curse of rage, threw down on the doctor.

Carson and Claiborne fired almost together. Claiborne s bullet went wide. The heavy slug from Carson's Colt smashed Claiborne's gun hand and knocked his six spinning across the room. As Carson's barrel lined with Ike Clanton, the latter threw down his gun and yelled for mercy.

Carson gestured with his gun barrel to the back door of the gallery.

" Get out," he ordered tersely.

" They'll kill us if we go out there! " wailed Clanton.

" They won't see yuh till yuh're too far away to hit," Carson said. " Get out, while yuh're able to walk."

One look at the doctor's bleak face and icy eyes was enough for Clanton. He slunk toward the back door, paused an instant and fled wildly for cover. Claiborne, moaning and cursing, and wringing his bloody hand, staggered after him.

Carson ran back to the front door. He saw Frank McLowery weaving about in the middle of the street, his face contorted with agony and rage. McLowery steadied himself and took deliberate aim at Doc Holliday. Holliday turned sideways and shot at the same instant.

Morgan Earp, who lay on the ground, knocked there by the shock of a slug fired by Billy Clanton that drilled his shoulder, also shot at McLowery.

McLowery pitched forward on his face, stone dead, a bullet through his brain. Who killed him, Holliday or Morgan Earp, was never determined.

A ball from Billy Clanton's gun cut through the calf of Virgil Earp's leg, bringing him to his knees. He and Billy Clanton shot it out on their knees. Clanton fell backward, tried to raise his gun once more but was too weak. He collapsed on the ground. The fight was over.

The smoke of the first shot fired had not altogether dissipated in the air. The entire thing had lasted less than one minute!

Carson crossed the street to where Pete Spence stood looking dazed and uncertain. Frank Stillwell was moaning and jerking with returning consciousness.

Carson handed Spence his gun, muzzle first.

" Get Stillwell on his feet and trail yore rope," he told Spence. Suddenly he shot an inspired remark at the killer.

" And when yuh see Jim Hill the next time, tell him I wish I'd been on the Bisbee stage the night he helped yuh hold it up! "

Spence stared at him, jaw dropping.

" How—how'd yuh know—" he stuttered. Then, with a muffled oath, he clamped his mouth shut tight. He glared at Carson, turned and bent over the writhing Stillwell. Carson deliberately turned his back on him and crossed the street.

Tom and Frank McLowery lay dead in the dust. Billy Clanton was being carried upstairs to Doc Goodfellow's office. He was still alive but going fast. The Earps, Virgil leaning on Doc Holliday's arm, Morgan supported by Wyatt, were heading back to town.

Carson joined them. He took Virgil and Morgan into his office and treated their wounds, which were ugly but not particularly serious.

"Well we won the fight, anyhow," Morgan asserted with a wry smile.

" Yes," Tom Carson replied quietly, " and lost it."

Wyatt Earp stared at the young doctor.

" Son, I've a notion yuh're plumb right," he said.

Chapter 12

TOM CARSON was right. Tragedy followed tragedy in quick succession. Marshal Virgil was shot from ambush and seriously wounded. His injuries left him a cripple and he resigned his office. Then one night Morgan Earp was playing pool in Campbell and Hatch's saloon and billiard hall on Allen Street between Fourth and Fifth. Bullets crashed through the glass panes of a door leading onto an alley. Morgan Earp fell, mortally wounded. He died less than an hour later. As Wyatt Earp, hastily summoned to the scene, bent over him, Morgan whispered something in his ear. Wyatt Earp straightened up, gazed down at his dead brother. His face was set in granite lines. His grey eyes were like wind-swept winter ice. On that grim face vengeance was written.

It was pretty well proven that Frank Stillwell, Pete Spence and Indian Charlie Cruz were guilty of the murder. All had arranged alibis in advance, and had not Pete Spence had a quarrel with his Mexican wife and slapped her face, they might have escaped direct suspicion. As it was, before he left Tombstone with his brother's body, Wyatt Earp knew the identity of his assassins.

Wyatt Earp killed Frank Stillwell and Indian Charlie Cruz. But the power of the Earps in Tombstone was broken. They had been four fighting men closely banded together. Now they were but two, and with the departure of crippled Virgil Earp for California, they lost the prestige of police power. It was time for them to leave Tombstone, and they knew it. They took their time about it, winding up their affairs, saying good-bye to friends and associates. They shipped their effects out of the country. Warren Earp, a younger brother, Sherman McMasters, Texas Jack Vermillion and Jack Johnson decided to accompany Wyatt and Doc Holliday on the outbound trail. At the last moment, Sheriff Behan attempted to arrest Wyatt Earp and Doc Holliday for the killing of Frank Stillwell. Wyatt and Holliday did not choose to be arrested, and Sheriff Behan backed down.

Grim and alert, Wyatt Earp and his followers walked their horses out of town. Allen Street was lined with crowds. Faces banked at the kerbs silently watched the grim cavalcade ride northwestward. Many of those present hated the Earps and Doc Holliday. But there was no demonstration, no threats. Tom Carson and other friends of the Earps walked slowly along the street, tense and watchful. They paused at the edge of town, but the six horsemen, with never a backward glance, rode on.

Tom Carson watched them go—Wyatt Earp to live out the full of his four score years, prosperous, honoured and respected; Warren Earp to fall before a gunman's bullet; Doc Holliday to die in bed, jesting with death, chuckling with grim humour over the perversity of fate that ruled that he should take the big jump with his boots off. He had offered odds of eight to five, in the old days, that despite the consumption from which he suffered, he would cash in at the business end of a sixshooter—and he lost his bet.

Westward the land was bright with sunshine; but to the east, dark and ominous clouds were rising, fold on fold. Slowly their sombre shadow crept over Tombstone—a portent of the doom that was soon to envelop the Silver City. The Dragoons stood sinister and mysterious, towering over the town, grim, implacable. The Tombstone Hills drew their drab pauper's mantle closer about them as the shadows deepened. They were all but ready to take back unto themselves their own. Even now their hidden, elemental forces were gathering for the blow that was to sweep the town clean of its bustle and colour and prosperity and pride.

Symbolical was the passing of that cavalcade of stern and daring men who had ruled the town at the height of its glory. In them was embodied the robust, unconquerable spirit of the West, the romance, the glamour, the vision of the Frontier.

With them was to pass the glory of the town they had ruled.

The clouds rolled onward, until the whole sky was one vast leaden arch. Tombstone lay swathed in gloom, obscured by drifting rain mists. Men went about their business thoughtfully, depressed.

Tom Carson walked slowly back to his little office through almost deserted streets. His eyes were sombre, his face set in deep lines. He was thinking deeply, formulating a plan of action. He passed Johnny Behan, and the little sheriff smirked maliciously. Carson could read his exultant thoughts. With the Earps gone, Tom Carson was very much on his own. But as the cold eyes of the tall young doctor met his, some of the exultation left Sheriff Behan.

"God! " he muttered to himself as he hurried on. " I thought for a minute Wyatt Earp was back lookin' at me! "

Jim Hill had apparently vanished from Tombstone and Cochise county. Carson had hung around Garcia's cantina considerably, in the hope that another of his half-breed henchmen would show up, but with barren results. Carson decided to play a hunch.

Pete Spence, after the killing of Morgan Earp, had fled to Sonora. By doing so, he escaped Earp vengeance. Carson, recalling the effect his random remark had had on Spence the day of the fight in the O.K. corral, was convinced that Jim Hill had been the mysterious third person in the Bisbee stage holdup. He had a hunch that where Spence was, there Jim Hill would also be. With the death of Stillwell and Indian Charlie, Spence was about the only one of the Cochise county outlaws left that Hill could team up with. John Ringo's enmity estranged Hill from Curly Bill Graham and his associates. Stillwell and Pete Spence had always been more of the lone wolf type and had worked by themselves. They had never been a real part of Curly Bill's close-knit organization. Carson did some careful planning and resolved on a course of action.

It was past midnight and still raining when Carson rode out of town. Gone were the fashionable, becoming clothes and careful grooming of young Doctor Carson of Tombstone. They were replaced by the careless but efficient and picturesque garb of the rangeland—soft blue shirt, vivid handkerchief looped about his sinewy throat, faded overalls, batwing chaps, scuffed boots and battered " J.B.". His heavy double cartridge belts encircled his lean waist and from the carefully worked and oiled cut-out holsters protruded the black butts of his long Colts. His well used rope hung from the saddle bow; there was a compact cooking outfit and a store of provisions in his blanket roll. His Winchester snugged in the saddle boot.

In fact Doctor Carson had, to all appearances, ceased to exist. His place was taken by Tom Carson, chuck-line ridin' cowpoke on the move once more. The only thing reminiscent of Doctor Carson was the little black medicine and instrument case that lay in the blanket roll alongside the cooking outfit.

South by west Carson rode through the cold drizzle and the moaning wind. Dawn found him threading his way through the canyon where he had trailed the Yaqui breed to Jim Hill's hangout. He entered the second canyon and cautiously passed the lonely prospector's cabin, wherein he had his last glimpse of Hill. No smoke rose from the chimney, now, and the front door sagged open on its rusty hinges.

Carson continued to ride, all that day and the next, until he passed through the gloomy gorge in the beetling cliff. Early that morning he had observed the " smoke talk " of the Yaquis staining the blue of the sky, and he knew he was closely watched by the mountain tribesmen. Unperturbed, however, he continued to ride in leisurely fashion. He had little doubt that his identity was already established by Quijano's young men who had him under surveillance. He was not in the least surprised when the old chief himself met him at the further mouth of the gorge.

Clinging to Quijano's hand was his small son, erect and sturdy, his false leg unnoticeable under his long buckskins.

Quijano greeted Carson warmly. Together they walked to the chief's cabin.

" You are most welcome, Señor," he said. " I hope you will stay long with us."

"I'd like to stick around till I grow a few whiskers," Carson replied.

" Ah," the chief replied quietly, " so you still seek for the the man Hill."

" That's right," Carson agreed. He detailed an account of Pete Spence's recent activities, for the Yaqui's benefit.

" Spence was last heard of down in Sonora, in Magdalena," he concluded. " As soon as I get a little brush on my face so there'll be less chance of me being recognized, I'm going to try and get a line on Spence. I'm just about certain he'll lead me to Hill, sooner or later. I figure I can locate Spence down here somewhere."

" I have a better plan," Quijano replied. " While you wait here, I will dispatch some of my young men to Magdalena. They will try and learn of the man Spence. It will be simpler for them than for you. Their presence there will excite no comment, and they have friends in Magdalena."

" That's mighty fine of yuh, Chief," Carson said gratefully. " I've a notion yuh've got the right idea. Spence is liable to be mighty suspicious of any Americano who shows up in the section. He wouldn't notice yore men. Tell them if there happens to be a stage line worth robbing anywhere in the section they'll find Spence hanging around. That's his specialty. He and Frank Stillwell robbed the stages so often up in Arizona that the drivers got to know him by his voice! "

He gave Quijano a careful description of Spence. The chief passed it on to three of his most trusted followers, who immediately departed for Magdalena, many miles to the south.

Nearly two weeks passed, pleasantly enough for Carson, before the young men returned.

" A man answering the description you gave us has been seen in Magdalena," they told the chief. " Also, a prospector there was recently murdered and robbed of his gold. A smuggling train was attacked by three masked men and looted.

The rurales are riding in search of the robbers, but with no success."

"That'll be Spence and some of his breeds," Carson declared with conviction. "And I've a mighty good notion that Jim Hill is one of the three men who held up the smugglers. Spence and Hill used to work with Curly Bill Graham, and smuggling trains were allus Curly Bill's meat. He massacred one in Skeleton Canyon, in Arizona, killed nineteen Mexicans and got seventy-five thousand dollars. One Mexican boy escaped. Later he led a band who killed Old Man Clanton and others who took part in the massacre, which included three of the Mexican boy's brothers."

Tom Carson rode away from the Yaqui village the following morning. Hardly had he passed from sight when Quijano summoned his three young men who had scouted Magdalena.

"Follow," he ordered tersely. "Follow—and assist if necessary."

The three tribesmen nodded silently and left the patriarch's presence.

Chapter 13

IN the hills close to the pueblo of Magdalena was an American owned silver mine, a good producer, though small. Its stamp mill was also small, but efficiently operated. The mine was a paying proposition.

The night of the monthly clean-up the stamps were silent. The workmen were in town enjoying a little hard earned recreation. The gaunt building was silent and deserted. It was dark save for a single lamp that burned in the mine office.

In the office, seated around a table, were three men. One was the American manager of the mine. Another was the Mexican superintendent. The third was the watchman, who was eating his lunch.

Manager and superintendent were busy poring over sheets covered with figures. Across from the desk stood a tall iron safe, the door locked. Stored in the safe was the monthly clean-up, hefty ingots of silver with a high gold content. They would be taken to Magdalena the following morning for shipment.

The watchman half dozed over his coffee. The two officials busied themselves over their totals, absorbed in their task. None of the trio heard the outer door open softly. The sudden flaring of the lamp in the draught brought their heads up.

In the open doorway stood a tall masked man. Close beside him pressed two other of slighter build.

The manager leaped to his feet, reaching toward a drawer. Something like a flickering lance of flame hissed across the room. The manager fell back with a gurgling cry, a long knife buried to the hilt in his throat. He crashed to the floor, taking his overturned chair with him. A gun in the left hand of the tall masked man menaced his companions.

" Stay put or yuh'll get the same thing," the knife thrower growled harshly.

130

The superintendent understood the English words; the watchman did not; but both understood perfectly the menace of that black gun muzzle.

The killer singled out the superintendent for attention. He gestured toward the safe with his gun barrel.

" Get over there and open that," he ordered.

The superintendent met the deadly threat of the pale eyes glaring through the mask holes. Tremblingly he got slowly to his feet. He crossed the room and began working the combination of the safe. A moment later he swung the door open.

The tall outlaw grunted as the lamplight gleamed on the rows of silver bricks stacked in the safe. He gestured to his followers, who immediately began removing the bricks and carrying them outside. It took them some time to clean the safe of its contents. The tall leader stood to one side, gun in hand, alert and watchful. When the last ingot had been removed, he turned to the two Mexicans.

" Stay right where yuh are, if yuh know what's good for yuh," he said. " One move and yuh get it."

Then he, too, vanished through the outer door, closing it after him.

The two men left in the office remained motionless until they heard the click of hoofs fading into the distance. Another moment and the outlaws had vanished beyond hearing, bearing with them more than fifty thousand dollars worth of silver.

It took three days' riding for Tom Carson to reach Magdalena. From the crest of a tall hill, just as the sun was sinking in scarlet and gold behind the western crags he saw the muddle of buildings, misty with distance, that formed the town. For a few minutes he sat his tall roan, outlined against the sky, and gazed toward the pueblo. Then he sent the cayuse down the winding, brush-flanked trail that led to it. Several miles farther on he rounded a sharp bend and came face to face with a dozen mounted men who appeared to have been awaiting his approach. They were armed with rifle, revolver and machete, and by their garb Carson recognized them as a squadron of El Presidente's rurales—mounted police. He drew rein and waited for them to speak.

An officer sat his horse a few paces in front of his men. He held up his hand.

"Señor," he asked politely, "from where do you come?"

"From Arizona," Carson replied.

"You have not been in these parts before?"

Carson shook his head. "Just rode down," he replied. "Never been in this section before."

"And what is your business here?"

"Oh, nothing in pertickler," Carson said. "Thought mebbe I could tie onto a job of riding hereabouts. I understand there are American-owned spreads in this section."

"That is true," the officer admitted, adding, "It is a long ride you have taken, Señor, just to look for employment. I have been told that good vaqueros are scarce from where you come. Why ride such a distance to seek that which could be found at home, Señor?"

"Oh, just itchy feet, I reckon," Carson evaded. "Sorta took a notion to see the country down here."

The officer stared at him, appeared to consider, to come to a decision.

"Señor," he said, "you will come with us."

"Why?" Carson asked.

"That matters not. It is an order," the officer replied coldly. "You will please to raise your hands, and keep them raised while my men secure your arms. At once, Señor!"

There was nothing for Carson to do but obey. To offer resistance was tantamount to suicide. Besides, these men were duly accredited officers of the law, and from such, he felt, he had nothing to fear. He raised his hands shoulder high and sat motionless while his guns were unbuckled and his Winchester removed from the boot. Then, at a gesture from the officer, he rode forward. Two rurales took up a position on either side of him and the cavalcade headed for Magdalena through the gathering dusk.

In front of the office of the alcalde—the mayor—the rurales

halted. Carson was ordered to dismount. Closely guarded he entered the building.

In the alcalde's office, the mayor, a cold-eyed, sharp-featured man, was seated behind a table desk. With him were a well dressed efficient looking Mexican of good quality, and a second man in peon's garb. All three wore an air of expectancy. And all three keenly scrutinized the prisoner.

" Well? " the alcalde asked, turning to the first of his companions.

The well dressed man hesitated, peering at Carson, running his glance over him carefully from head to foot.

" This one is of the same height, I would say, and the clothes appear to be the same," he remarked. " The face of the bandit was masked, but otherwise I would say they are indeed much the same, in build and general appearance."

The peon nodded emphatic corroboration of all the other said.

The alcalde regarded Carson with his cold eyes. He turned and questioned the captain of the rurales, who detailed his initial encounter with Carson, repeating the answers to his questions one by one.

Again the alcalde turned his attention to Carson. For some moments he said nothing. Then he apparently made up his mind.

" Señor," he said, " I will be forced to detain you in confinement for a while. A more thorough investigation of your movements and your past is imperative."

" Just what am I accused of? " Carson asked, breaking silence for the first time.

" Of the robbery of the Sitic silver mine and the murder of its manager," the alcalde replied in cold tones. He raised his hand as Carson started to speak.

" That will be all for the present, Señor," he said with finality. " Tomorrow you will be given a further hearing."

He turned to the captain of the rurales and waved his hand toward the door.

" Place his arms and other belongings here in the office, and tie his caballo in the shed behind the building," he directed.

Carson's guns, rifle and riding gear were deposited in a corner. A rurale led his horse away. Again the alcalde gestured with his hand.

A mounted policeman took Carson, by either arm. The captain motioned to the door.

And in the darkness beyond the open window, hard black eyes watched every move, and ears as sharp as a dog's heard every word that was spoken.

Fifteen minutes later Tom Carson was securely locked up in the town calaboose.

The calaboose was a small building perched on the bank of a stream that ran past the western outskirts of the town. The rear of the building overhung the stream and was supported by two stout posts. The front was level with the street. A small outer room furnished with a table, chairs and a bunk built against the wall was reserved for the accommodation of the jailer, who evidently slept in the building. Beyond was an iron door which shut off a corridor and three small cells. All were vacant at the present. Carson was ushered into one and the cell door and the outer door were locked behind him.

There was a low bunk that took up more than half of the cell space, and no other furnishings. The end wall of the cell was pierced by a window that looked out upon the dark waters of the stream. It was barred with upright iron bars set into the wooden frame of the window, which was devoid of glass. There were no lighting arrangements in the cell room, and when the outer door was closed, the place was pitch dark save for a gleam of moonlight that reflected from the water below.

His tobacco and papers had been left to him, so Carson sat down on the bunk and rolled a cigarette, which he smoked thoughtfully gazing through the window toward the far bank of the stream, which was clothed in a straggle of growth.

Carson knew he was in a very tight spot. He was familiar enough with the workings of Mexican courts to realize that the evident suspicions of the Mexican mine official were just about sufficient evidence to secure his conviction, which would probably mean an adobe wall and a firing squad. The best he could hope for, if the court adjudged him guilty, was a long term in prison, and a long term in a Mexican prison was to an American usually the equivalent of a death sentence.

The only explanation he had to offer for his presence in the section would sound fantastic, he was forced to admit. To make matters worse, he dared not refer the alcalde to Tombstone and his connections there. He grimly visualized Sheriff Behan's reply to such a request. The sheriff's expressed opinion of him would be the same as a death warrant.

Yes, things looked mighty bad, but with a shrug, Carson stretched out on the bunk, pillowed his head on his hands and proceeded to take it easy. Perhaps something would turn up to swing the balance in his favour. If it didn't—well, there was no use to worry about it; worrying wouldn't make things any better.

Arrived at this decision, he dozed comfortably, while the moon slanted down the sky and the water of the stream grew black with shadow.

It was past midnight when Carson was suddenly aroused by a slight sound. For a moment he lay at a loss as to what it was. Then it resolved into a slight but persistent scratching at the window bars of his cell. He listened a moment longer, then arose noiselessly and glided to the window. The moon was low in the sky now, its rays striking on the straggle of brush beyond the narrow stream; but enough starlight filtered down to outline a shadowy face at the window. As Carson approached, a voice breathed out of the darkness:

" It is Kepnau," said the voice.

Kepnau, Carson recalled, was the elder of the three young men Quijano, the chief, had sent to Magdalena to ferret out information concerning Pete Spence's whereabouts.

" What in blazes are you doing here, Kepnau?" he whispered back.

" Listen, Señor," Kepnau replied. " I have ropes. I will tie them to the window bars. Hidden in the growth beyond the stream are Mukwarrah and Quajas, with the other ends of the ropes secured to the horses. We will jerk the bars free. You must come quickly through the opening and wade the stream—it is not deep. We have your horse awaiting you. The jailer sleeps. He will not hear until it is too late. Make ready, Señor. I have fastened the ropes."

Another instant and the face vanished.

"That hellion must have feet like a lizard's to swarm up the piling that way and get hold of the window bars," Carson chuckled under his breath. Standing a little back from the window, he waited, tense and ready.

Minutes passed, then Carson heard the slight hum of the tightening ropes. The window bars creaked, the woodwork of the frame complained with a low groaning. Carson gathered himself together for the scramble through the window.

The creaking grew louder. The ropes suddenly hummed like harp strings. With a rending, splintering sound the bars ripped free from the window frame.

But the noise of their loosening was drowned in a prodigious crackle and crash. Carson gripped the window ledge with both hands as the floor tilted crazily under his feet. His body swung wildly through the air, his grip was torn loose and he seemed to turn a complete somersault in the air to land with stunning force, not on the floor, but on the rough boards of the low ceiling!

Chapter 14

FOR an instant Carson lay half stunned. The last thing he recalled hearing was a most prodigious splash, and an unearthly yell from the outer room. Then, his head still whirling, he scrambled to his feet. The window opening was above him, barely within reach of his clutching hands.

" Good Lord! " he gasped, " The piling busted and the jail-house turned clean over and landed in the crik! "

In the outer room beyond the cells the yells continued, and a frantic scrambling. Carson clawed his way up the sloping wall, gained the opening and levered his body through. As he dropped into the water, the horses of Kepnau, Mukwarrah and Quapas boiled across the stream in his direction. He scrambled erect, spluttering and gasping; a brown hand was reached down to him.

"Up, Señor, up! " bawled Kepnau. In an instant Carson was astride the cayuse behind him and Kepnau was turning the horse's head toward the far bank.

From the front of the overturned jail sounded a booming report.

" What the jailer shoot at—feesh? " Quapas asked.

" You will know what he shoot at, stupid one, if we are not in the bushes before he gets around to this side," whooped Kepnau. " Vamos, muy pronto! "

Through the shallow water surged the frantic horses. They scrambled and floundered up the slippery bank. From across the stream came a red flash of flame and again the boom of a shotgun. Buckshot stormed through the bushes above their head. But before the cursing, bellowing jailer could reload a second time, they tore through the growth and out of his sight.

Once in the brush, Kepnau diagonalled sharply to the left. Another moment and by a vagrant beam of moonlight Carson

saw his big roan, saddled and bridled, tethered to a branch.
His Winchester was in the saddleboot, and over the horn hung
his belts and sixguns.

"The alcalde is doubtless angry," Kepnau observed reflect-
ively as they headed away from town at a gallop. "We tied
him to his chair and the cords were tight, and by this time
uncomfortable."

"And he'll need a new jail too," Carson chuckled. "When
you fellers go in for jail delivery yuh do a thorough chore."

"But yuh sure pulled me out of a tough spot," he added
gratefully. "Things were beginning to look as dark as the
inside of a black bull in fly time. How come you fellers showed
up at such a good time?"

"Quijano told us to follow, and assist if necessary," Kepnau
replied simply. "Our Father forgets not those who have
favoured him."

"Well, what I was able to do for him sure came back, and
brought plenty with it," Carson said. "It looked for a while
they were going to tie that job of robbery and killing onto me.
I've a prime notion, Kepnau, that job was pulled off by Pete
Spence and his outfit."

"That is so," Kepnau replied. "After listening outside the
alcalde's window and learning what was to be done with you,
we visited a friend who has a cantina in this town. There we
waited till all were asleep, and while we waited we talked with
our amigo, who knows much of what goes on. He told us
that it was the man Spence and two of his half white, half-Indio
companions who robbed the mine. Also, Señor, he told us
where those men are to be found."

Kepnau paused significantly. Carson turned quickly in his
saddle.

"He did!" he exclaimed. "Can yuh really locate them,
Kepnau?"

"Si," Kepnau replied. "To the place where they are to be
found we ride even now."

Carson had already realized that they were following a
distinct trail in the course of their flight from the town.

"Si," Kepnau repeated. " We know the place, Señor, and if you wish, we will pause there for a short time."

There was a grim note in the Yaqui's voice, and in the faint moonlight that still followed along the plane of the horizon, Carson could see that his dark face was set like stone.

" Lead on, feller," Carson said, " mebbe we'll have a show-down this time."

The trail, which had been flowing almost due west abruptly curved to the south. Another hour of riding and a faint grey in the west heralded the dawn. The moon had sunk behind the crags and the night was very dark. Kepnau slackened the pace.

Another ten minutes and in the strengthening light, Carson saw a small huddle of silent buildings.

" Here live honest folks who till the soil and tend their herds," Kepnau said in low tones. " Beyond is a place where evil men congregate.. Our amigo of the cantina told us that the men we seek plan to leave that place with the first light. Perhaps they will not leave after all."

Carson nodded agreement to the old finality in the Yaqui's voice.

They rode on through the silent village, until they reached the edge of a grove.

" Here we will leave the caballos," said Kepnau.

They dismounted, and stole forward through the gloom under the wide spreading branches of the trees. It did not take them long to pass through the grove. On the far edge was a squat building with a door and a single dirty window facing the grove. A light glowed in the building. From the edge of the grove to the door was but a few paces.

Tensely, Carson and his Yaqui followers crouched in the gloom under the trees and surveyed the cabin. Once or twice a shadow passed across the window. Evidently the occupants were up and moving about.

" Nothing to be gained by waiting," Carson said at length. " Come on—hit the door hard, and be ready for anything."

Shoulder to shoulder they raced across the narrow clearing. Carson's muscular body crashed against the door with splintering force.   There was a screech of rending wood and metal, the door flew wide open, banging against the wall.   Carson and his Yaquis stormed into the room.

With startled yells, three men leaped from a table at which they had been eating.   One was Pete Spence.   The others were swarthy breeds with lowering, evil countenances.

Pete Spence's hand flickered down and up.   His draw was unbelievably fast.   His gun spouted fire the same instant that Carson's Colts boomed thunderously in the close room.

A lock of black hair leaped from the side of Carson's head. Something twitched at his shirt sleeve like an urgent hand.   Then Pete Spence reeled backward with a choking cry, overturning the table and hitting the floor with a clatter of breaking dishes.

The two breeds were also blazing away, the flashes of their guns stabbing the murk of the smoke filled room.   But the Yaquis were shooting hard and fast.   Under the murderous volley of their rifles the breeds went down, riddled with bullets.

Through the swirling smoke wreaths, Carson walked across the room, shoved the table aside and leaned over Pete Spence. Spence was shot through the chest and a glance told Carson that he was going fast.   He squatted beside the dying outlaw. Spence glared up at him.   Recognition blazed in his filming eyes.

" Carson! " he gasped.

" Yes, it's me," Carson told him.   He stared at the owlhoot.

" Pete," he said, " yuh're going to take the big jump.   Make it easier for yourself and come clean.   Where's Jim Hill? "

The terror of death and the hereafter was numbing the outlaw's soul.

" Do something for me, Carson, do somethin' for me! " he gurgled through the blood welling in his throat.

" I'll do what I can for yuh, Pete," Carson promised. " Where's Jim Hill? "

" Tombstone," gasped Spence.   " Tombstone."

" Where in Tombstone? " Carson asked as he began cutting away Spence's blood soaked shirt.

" Sul—sul—" gurgled Spence.   The blood flooded in his throat and frothed over his lips.   He choked, gasped, coughed spasmodically. His chest arched mightily as he fought for air. It sank in until it looked almost hollow, and did not rise again. Pete Spence stiffened, relaxed. His glazed eyes stared straight upward rigidly fixed in death.

His face etched in bitter lines, Tom Carson rose to his feet and gazed down at the dead outlaw.

" 'Sul—sul'," he repeated Spence's last words. " Now what in blazes did he mean by that? "

Still pondering the riddle of the meaningless syllables, he ejected the spent shells from his guns and replaced them with fresh cartridges.

The Yaquis were prowling about, inside the building and out. Mukwarrah stuck his head in through the door.

" Señor," he called, " there are mules in a shed behind the cabin. They bear aparejos—pack saddles—and the aparejos are filled with much silver."

" The loot from the Sitic mine," Carson said. " Okay fellers help me carry these bodies out and tie them onto the backs of the mules."

" Where do we take them," Kepnau asked as he and Quapas seized a dead breed, head and heels.

" To Magdalena," Carson replied briefly.

The alcalde of Magdalena was in a very bad temper indeed. He sat at his desk, chafing his still numbed and sore wrists. He had spent many hours tied to his chair, and he had liked it not at all. He mumbled curses to himself, and from time to time glared out of the window. He raised his head at a clatter of hoofs outside that ceased in front of his office. Then he half rose from his chair, and sank back, his lips whitening as he stared at the tall figure framed in the doorway. Behind Tom Carson showed the grim faces of his Yaquis.

" Señor!" gasped the Alcalde, " you return! Wh-why? What wish you? "

" Come here—outside," Carson ordered tersely.

The alcalde rose on trembling legs and obeyed. He shrank as far away as possible from the sinister quartette as he sidled through the door.

Clustered in front of his office were a number of mules bearing well filled pack saddles. Three of the animals, in addition, had motionless bodies draped across their backs.

"There are the men who robbed the mine, and there is the silver they stole," Carson said.

"But—but, Señor, I do not understand!" faltered the alcalde.

Carson gestured to the body of Pete Spence.

"Listen," he said. "I rode down here from Arizona looking for that man, and another one. I found this one. Now I'm heading back for Arizona for the other. I want a safe conduct from you in case I run into some of yore rurales on the way back. I don't want to have any trouble with them. Write it out, will yuh?"

"Of a certainty, Señor," the alcalde said hastily. "You have done me a great service, though your methods are somewhat peculiar."

He seated himself at his desk. His pen scratched busily for several minutes.

"Here, Señor," he said at length, passing the document to Carson. "I am sure you will find this satisfactory."

Carson glanced over the lines.

"Fine," he said. "Yuh sure did it up brown, all right. This had oughta get us into El Presidente's palace, if we wanted to go there. Gracias."

"But wait, Señor," called the alcalde as Carson turned to depart. "Wait! There is a large reward offered by the Sitic Mining Company for the apprehension of those ladrones and the return of the stolen silver. It is yours by all rights."

"Keep it," Carson returned. He smiled slightly for the first time.

"Use it to build yuh a new jailhouse," he chuckled, "and divide what's left among yore rurales. They struck me as good fellows. Adios."

The alcalde stared through the window at the stern figures riding swiftly toward the northern hills.

"Madre de Dios" (Mother of God) "Have mercy on that 'other one'!" he breathed.

Chapter 15

TOM CARSON sojourned a week in Quijano's village; then he returned to Tombstone. His heavy beard had now grown to quite a respectable length. The bronze of his face was darker. His clothes and riding gear showed signs aplenty of hard usage. Altogether, there was little to remind of the immaculate young doctor who had walked the streets of the silver town a month before.

Tombstone was booming. The town didn't know it, but it was the last hectic fever-flush of coming dissolution, the bright flaring of a lamp with the oil-of-life burned to the dregs, the final brilliant glow before the smoky flicker and darkness. In the murky depths of the great silver mines, forces were gathering, vast, elemental forces that no ingenuity of man could defeat. The prisoned powers of earth-heart were about to be loosed in terror and fury, irresistible, supernal, to sweep to nothingness the fruits of man's labour, and to render futile for all time his apparent conquest of his vast treasure house of the hills. Tombstone roared to the stars, flaunting iniquities in the face of the inscrutable Heavens, secure in her smug complacency, careless of the present, heedless of the future, sneering at the calm, majestic countenance of Destiny enthroned beyond the spheres. And the dark powers beneath the granite bases of the mountains waited; while in the mine depths the " moving finger " wrote in unreadable hieroglyphics the doom of Tombstone, upon the glistening walls of stone.

Tombstone was at the high tide of its prosperity. Allen Street, a thoroughfare of stately width, roared with traffic. Wagon trains loaded with lumber rumbled in from the sawmills in the Chiricahuas and the Huachucas. It was needed, and more, too, for the new buildings going up in every direction. From the O. K. corral at one end to the Bird Cage Opera

House at the other, Allen Street was a solid double line of business houses of frame, brick and adobe. The buildings were mostly one-storey, but there was a fair sprinkling of two-storey "sky-scrapers." The sidewalks were sheltered from the sun by projecting roofs, and in their cool shade jostled a swarming multitude.

There were mine workers in blue, red or checkered shirts, cowboys in their picturesque garb of the range, storekeepers in broadcloth, gamblers in funeral black relieved only by the snow of their shirt fronts. Mexicans in velvet adorned by much silver rubbed shoulders with blanketed Indians and gaudily apparelled "ladies" of the dance halls. Respectable citizens and outlaws from the Dragoons peered into shop windows or stopped at the Oriental, the Crystal Palace or the Alhambra for a drink.

These saloons of Tombstone, and many others, were not places where roughly garbed oldtimers bellied the bar and bawled for hard likker. The great mirror blazing back bars were banked with bottles of many hues and containing all kinds of fancy drinks. A glass of straight whiskey reposed beside a tumbler of champagne. Fiery tequila and pousse-café's jostled rims and were downed with equal avidity by patrons of widely divergent tastes. "Name yore pizen" meant taking a choice of a great variety of potables. The barkeeps wore white aprons, there were paintings on the walls, the bar rails were of brass and the bar itself was very often real mahogany.

But despite this veneer of culture, the throngs that jostled and wrangled were the "frontier," be their garb broadcloth and fine linen or blue denim and rough wool. There were polished boots, and scuffed "high-heels" jingling spurs; but inside both were itchy feet that had strode into Tombstone in search of adventure, excitement, opportunity. The wearers were of that same robust breed that found even the wide circle of the horizon all too narrow for the sturdy spirit that was in them. Were their talents turned to good or bad, they were virile, ambitious, lusty of life. They shot their arrows to the sun, and if the charred sticks fell back upon their own heads, they took their wounds with a shrug, and went seeking more arrows.   They were the Southwest, the seekers after new things, the believers in opportunity, the pick of the world's glorious ones, be they sturdy saints or glorious sinners.

There was little difference between night and day in Tombstone in those days.   The saloons and gambling houses never closed, and the crowds were always there, be it high noon or midnight.   Fortunes were won on the turn of a card or the click of the ivory ball in a roulette wheel.   A hundred dollars for a white chip in a poker game was not uncommon.   Money was just something to get rid of.   The wealth of the Tombstone hills was inexhaustible, or so thought Tombstone.   And strange to say, Tombstone was to never exhaust the vast treasure.   There was to be no petering out, no gradual fading, no slow transition from roaring prosperity to drab pauperism. For Tombstone the sun was to set at noon, the clock was to stop even while striking the hour.

Bearded, spurred, in his well-worn range clothes, Tom Carson roamed the streets of Tombstone, no different from many another hard ridin' cowpoke in town for diversion.   He attracted no attention, and he was not recognized, even when he dropped into the Oriental for a drink with Buckskin Frank Leslie, the genial bartender, who looked harmless and respectable in his immaculate white coat and apron as his slim, deadly hands polished glasses with the same dexterity with which he " polished off " opponents with his ivory-handled sixguns.

Carson attended performances at the Bird Cage, the famous old honky tonk at the end of Allen Street, where the audience downed beers and whiskeys in a haze of tobacco smoke and vociferously applauded the efforts of the vaudeville performers behind the oil-lamp footlights.   He bucked the games at the Alhambra, downed fiery tequila in Garcia's sinister little cantina down on the stony claws of the lion's paw, watched Tombstone's " ladies of the evening " in their scanty costumes drinking at the bars or playing roulette in the Crystal Palace. He threaded his way through the mazes of cribs, tough saloons

K

and dance halls of that dubious quarter adjoining the business district encompassed by Allen, Fremont and Tough Nut Streets, listened to the music of Mexican Orchestras and more than once sniffed the smoke of six-shooters.

But nowhere did he see the face of the man he sought. Jim Hill was in Tombstone, Pete Spence had said with his dying words, and Carson believed him. But Hill was sure keeping under cover.

Often Carson pondered those enigmatical syllables that had choked out through the blood in Spence's throat—" Sul sul—! " What in blazes could they mean! He tried to tie them up with something definite, but could not. But nevertheless he firmly believed the key to Hill's whereabouts lay in those apparently meaningless expressions.

As a last resort, Carson began looking for places the name of which began with " Sul." He found several, but in none of them did he find Jim Hill.

" I'm beginning to think Pete Spence was either a liar or plumb loco," he declared in exasperation. But nevertheless he persisted in his fruitless search, all unaware that the dark powers imprisoned in the hills were preparing to lend a sardonic hand.

Chapter 16

FAR back in a tunnel of the Sulphuret mine, a tall, beardless miner swung his pick against a wall of veined and shattered rock. Fragments showered down under the attack of his lusty blows, clattering about his feet. He paused to wipe his heated brow and peer at the results of his labours by the light of his cap lamp. Half a dozen companions also paused a moment, breathing hard from their strenuous labours in the close air.

After a breathing spell, they again attacked the wall, the tall man, who held the position of straw-boss over the gang, leading and directing operations.

For some time the fragments showered down. The face of the wall glistened with moisture. Little whorls and scrawls formed from the trickling drops—strange, inscrutable writings that seemed to take on definite form.

Again the tall, beardless man stepped back. Setting his pick against the side wall, he proceeded to roll a cigarette, deftly, swiftly, using only the fingers of his left hand. His companions emulated his example, but they handled tobacco and papers in clumsy fashion with blunt, broken-nailed fingers thick with callouses of many years of hard rock work.

The tall man inhaled a lungful of smoke, blew it out, and thoughtfully contemplated the glistening face of the rock.

" She's gettin' almighty wet in this drift," he observed. "I've a notion they're goin' to have a job of pumpin' to do before they're finished with."

" Got a notion yuh're right, Highpockets," a fellow workman agreed. " It's been gettin' wetter right along."

Highpockets carefully pinched out the butt of his cigarette before dropping it to the damp floor. He hitched his cap over one eye, seized his pick and stepped up to the wall. He

147

swung the pick lustily and brought it down against the stone. The point wedged fast in a crevice. He tried to wrench it free, and could not. He swore at the stubborn rock and put forth his strength in a mighty effort.

The pick came free, and as it did so, the crevice suddenly widened and lengthened to cover the whole face of the wall. A huge slab of rock leaned slowly outward, as if projected by force from behind.

The tall man leaped back with a warning shout. His companions scrambled for safety as the great slab thundered down to strike the floor with a reverberating crash.

After the slab came a jet of water thick as a man's wrist and hard as steel. It caught Highpockets full in the breast and knocked him backward a dozen feet. He reeled, scrambled, fell to the floor, spluttering curses. Dashing the drops from his eyes, he staggered to his feet, and stared at the rock wall.

A second jet had followed the first, a third, and a fourth. " Say," began Highpockets.

His voice was drowned in a shattering boom as the entire face of the wall dissolved and crashed down. Over the scattered fragments roared a torrent of water, icy-cold, black as ink.

With yells of fear the miners turned and fled along the corridor. After them thundered the icy flood. Fright lent wings to their feet, but run as they would the roaring water was faster. It sloshed about their feet, rose to their ankles, their knees, clutching and tearing at them, all but sweeping them off their feet. Mad to escape the terror ravening at their heels, they swerved into a side tunnel that sloped steeply upward, and which led, they knew, to the open air. Gasping and panting, they toiled up the steep incline. Behind them they could hear the water roaring down the main tunnel, the floor of which was pierced with shafts leading to the lower workings.

They could hear something else. Over their heads sounded ominous rumblings and groanings. The solid rock of the mountain seemed to be labouring in agony. The adamantine walls of the drift shuddered as with an earthquake. The floor rocked under their feet.

Louder and louder sounded the boomings and thuddings from the galleries above.

" The hull damn mine's cavin' in," gasped one of the men. " It's gonna—good God, look out! "

The huge timbers with which the drift was shored were buckling. The great squared beams were bending like bow staves. Earth and stones showered down. There was a sudden mighty roar, a long rumbling crash, through which knifed a scream of agony and terror.

The miners fled madly up the incline from the jagged barrier of stone and rubble and splintered timbering that stretched from wall to wall behind them. They raced upward, wild with fright, but only six instead of the seven that had dashed from the main drift. In the black dark that closed down as their winking cap lamps vanished from view there was silence broken only by the soft lap-lap of the rising water and a low, anguished moaning that sobbed from where the fallen roof blocked the tunnel.

Far up the drift the fleeing miners paused to catch their breath. As they grouped together against the quivering wall of the gallery, one suddenly uttered an exclamation—

" There's only six of us! Who—where—God! where's Highpockets? "

Mute with horror they stared into one another's white and scared faces.

" He—he must be under that stuff that fell ! " one quavered.

There was stunned silence, then a squat, broad miner spoke decisively. " We got to get him out," he said. " Come on, we're goin' back."

" The hull damn roof's liable to cave in any minute—we'll all be caught if it does," another quavered.

" Can't help it," said the first speaker. " We can't leave him down there unless we're sure he's done for. Come along! "

He turned and hurried down the gallery. The others

followed grimly, fully aware of the chances they were taking, but hesitating not at all.

Above ground the Sulphuret mill whistle burst into a long-continued roar as men began pouring out of the main tunnel of the upper level.   Soon other mine whistles on the hill began to boom.   The initial flood in the Sulphuret mine was but the first blow struck by the prisoned powers under the hills. Fettered forages, they were free at last.   The vast static forces, quiescent for untold centuries, had burst into raging kinetic energy.   Water was rising in all the mines.   It boiled in the shafts and tunnels in geyser spouts as thick as a man's body. Shoring buckled and crumpled.   Corridors caved in.   The drifts were choked with rubble through which the water surged and seethed.

Miners, many of them injured, streamed down the hill toward town.   They met and mingled with crowds of citizens travelling upward to the mines.   In the van were doctors and nurses, for there was much for them to do.

Tom Carson was in the Oriental sipping a drink, his hatbrim drawn low over his eyes, when the news of the catastrophe reached him.

" There are men all busted up, others half drowned," said the excited informant as a crowd quickly gathered around him.

Tom Carson listened and abruptly he forgot all about his quest and Jim Hill.   Tom Carson, chuck-line ridin' cowboy, ceased to exist.   In his place was Doctor Carson hearing and heeding the call to duty.

He raced to his office, unlocked it, procured all that he thought needful and hurried up the hill.

Other doctors were there ahead of him.   Carson had cast off his broad brimmed hat and they recognized him at once, despite his beard and welcomed him gladly.

" Plenty to do and not enough to do it," said Doctor Good-fellow, wiping his streaming face with a hand wet with the blood of an amputation.   " Get busy, Carson, that feller over there is goin' to die if somethin' isn't done to take care of his bleedin'."

Carson and Goodfellow were working near the tunnel mouth of the Sulphuret mine. From time to time low-pitched ominous rumblings sounded from the depths of the tortured mountain. The earth trembled beneath their feet, the air quivered to the mighty vibrations. The crackling of buckling shoring and the thud of falling masses of rock punctuated the continuous roar of rushing water.

"The lower drifts are filling up," Goodfellow said. "It's lucky this thing happened just at shift changing time. Otherwise there would have been hundreds trapped down at the five-hundred foot levels. As it is, I wouldn't be surprised if there are men still underground. Wonder how it is over at the Tough Nut and the Contention?"

Carson had just straightened his aching back from a job of setting and bandaging a broken leg when six men came rushing from the tunnel mouth. Their clothes were drenched, their faces streaked with mud and grime. Their eyes were wild. They glared about, then hurried to where the two doctors stood.

"There—there's a feller down below," one gulped. "He's caught under a fall. Rock on his arm. We tried to get the stuff off him and couldn't He ain't dead, but unless somethin's done mighty quick he's a goner. Rocks are still fallin' down there and the hull passage is liable to cave in any minute. We figger the only way to get him out is to cut off his arm. It's all smashed to hell, anyhow. Will one of you fellers take a chance? The roof's liable to fall in at any time, but I'll go along with yuh."

Doctor Goodfellow began assembling his instruments, but Tom Carson put him aside.

"It's a young man's chore, Doc," he said quietly. "You can do more good up here, with your skill and experience. I'll go down. So long."

The older doctor reached out and gripped his young colleague's hand.

"So long, Carson," he said quietly. "I'll carry on up here."

With a squat, powerfully built miner leading the way, Tom

Carson entered the tunnel. He had hastily donned a cap lamp borrowed from one of the miners. He adjusted the light and strode shoulder to shoulder with his guide. Soon the dark swallowed them up and the shadows were relieved only by the feeble glow of lamps.

Over a clutter of fallen debris they picked their way. Far back along the main drift tunnel they turned into a narrower gallery that sloped steeply down.

Here the destruction was more appalling. Some of the great vertical timbers of the shoring, eighteen inches square, were sunk into the massive horizontal timbers upon which they stood to a depth of three inches and more. Others were bowed outward, still others smashed and splintered. From time to time, rocks and rubbish still fell from above, and all the while there was a sinister groaning and creaking to tell of the earth and stone sinking and settling as the supports of the lower level were washed away. Some of the twelve-inch horizontal timbers, Carson noted, were compressed until they were only five inches thick! Mute evidence of the tremendous power and weight of the sinking stone that could squeeze a solid log together in such a way.

As they progressed, the chaos became even more complete. Soon they were stooping and bending under masses of earth and stone. Finally they had to go down on hands and knees and crawl.

"It's wuss than what it was when we came out," the miner panted. "I'm scairt we're too late to do anythin' for High-pockets. We got a mighty slim chance of gettin' back out ourselves. Shall we keep goin', Doc?"

"Trail yore rope, feller," Carson answered. "We'll see this thing through, one way or another. How much farther to go?"

They reached a point where the tunnel narrowed and lowered to a mere fox's burrow through the jumbled mass of earth and stone and splintered wood.

"It had oughta be about here," said the miner. "Listen?"

Carson strained his ears, and distinctly heard, from a little distance ahead, a low moaning. The miner heard it, too. He raised his voice.

" Are yuh there, Highpockets? " he called.

A feeble answer came back from the darkness:

" Yes, but things are gettin' wuss. The rock's settlin' down all around me."

The miner started to wriggle into the narrow aperture, but his massive chest and shoulders were too wide and thick to make it. He gave back, swearing profusely.

" I figger I can make it," Carson told him. " Let me try. I've got to get in there first, anyhow, if I'm to do anything. Say, there's water on the floor here! "

" It's risin' up the gallery! " gulped the miner. " If things weren't bad enough as it is! We'll be drowned if we ain't squashed! "

Gripping his instrument case tightly, Carson wormed his way into the narrow hole. Trickles of earth and drippings of water fell on him as he squirmed along. The air was thick and stifling, and damp with the dampness of a newly opened tomb. He sloshed through water and muck, bruised his hands and knees on sharp fragments of stone. But the sound of moaning steadily drew nearer.

Finally he saw the injured miner. He lay on his back, in a little arched hollow formed by earth and stone resting on the bowed and splintered timbers that had broken under the weight pressing upon them from above. His right arm was extended, and covered to above the elbow by a huge fragment of rock. He was conscious and his head rolled slowly from side to side. It steadied as Carson drew near, glittering black eyes wild with pain and fear, glinted toward the approaching doctor.

Carson shuffled close, found he could assume a crouching position in the little hollow. He steadied himself on one hand, leaned over and peered into the stricken man's face. The hairless cheeks were smeared with grime and black muck, which in the deceptive light of the flickering cap lamp looked like the first growth of a black beard.

Tom Carson stared, his breath caught sharply, his face grew black as chiselled granite, his grey eyes icily cold as the water that slowly rose about his knees. He looked closer, to make sure there was no mistake. His breath exhaled in a hissing pant. His lips framed a name in almost inaudible tones:

" Jim Hill! "

Chapter 17

JIM HILL stared up into the face that bent over him, and recognition was instantly mutual.

" Carson! " he gasped. " Good God! Carson! "

" Yes," Carson replied slowly, ". it's me. Looks like I've run yuh down at last, Hill. So that's what Pete Spence meant by 'Sul—Sul'! Tried to tell me yuh were working in the Sulphuret mine, covering up with a job of respectable work, like yuh did before. Things sorta caught up with you, eh, Hill? "

Jim Hill was yammering with agony and terror. His voice rose in a thin whisper as Carson half straightened up and drew back.

" Don't leave me, Carson! " he babbled frenziedly. " I know I did yuh wrong, but don't leave me to die alone—in the dark! In the dark! "

Tom Carson continued to stare down at the frantic, terror stricken outlaw and murderer. He said nothing, only stared with icy eyes in which was mirrored a grim satisfaction. Here was revenge indeed! Above him the labouring mountain groaned and muttered. Earth and fragments of stone showered down. The buckled timbers creaked loudly, threatening to give way at any moment. To free Hill and drag him to safety would take time. Carson knew he was risking his life every second he remained in the reeking hole. He was also risking that of the honest miner who waited at the other end of the burrow who would not leave to seek safety until his companion rejoined him. He, Carson, would be utterly justified in leaving the murderous reptile pinned under the stone to meet a fate he richly deserved. No man would hold it against him. Hill had coming to him what he would get.

And then suddenly it seemed to Carson that there was a

third figure there with them in the black dark, a tall gaunt figure with a lined and kindly face, with eyes wise in the ways of men, wise and tolerant and forgiving, filled with the understanding that comes to those who dedicate their lives to the service of their fellow men. In Tom Carson's ears rang a voice—

"A doctor's mission is to save life and alleviate suffering. No circumstance relieves him of that duty. Personal preference or convenience must never be allowed to stand in the way. He dedicates his life to the service of humanity, and in that service he must never be found wanting."

Tom Carson breathed deeply. He half turned to where it seemed the figure of the old dean of medicine stood. His gaze met only broken stone and reeking earth; but he nodded his head as if in acquiescence to a wisdom greater than his own. He turned back to the stricken outlaw.

"I'll try and get yuh out, Hill," he said quietly. "The only way is to take yore arm off. I can't get yuh loose any other way. I'm going to give yuh a hypodermic shot now. It may kill yuh, but I can't chance one of less strength. I think the pain yuh're suffering will keep yuh alive."

With steady hands he opened the instrument case, charged the hypodermic case with what would have been under any other circumstances a lethal dose of morphine and injected it. He waited a few minutes for the drug to take effect, while the icy water rose steadily around him and the trickles of dislodged earth and stone increased in volume. Then, working swiftly and surely, he cut flesh and sawed bone until the moaning but nearly unconcious Hill was freed from the mangled pulp imprisoned by the fallen rock. He tied the arteries, padded and bandaged the wound as well as he was able. He was shaking with strain and fatigue when the job was finished.

And yet his work was but half done. He still had to drag Hill's heavy body through the tortuous burrow before he could hope for assistance from the waiting miner at its far end.

Summoning his last reserves of strength, Carson began the task. For what seemed to him untold ages, he tugged and struggled with the flaccid form, gaining inch by slow inch, supporting Hill's face above the rising water with one arm and hauling at him with the other. Once a falling stone struck him a numbing blow on the head and he all but dropped senseless to drown with the outlaw in the dark. Red flashes were storming before his eyes, his head pounded as if a triphammer was beating against his brain, a hot iron band was tightening and tightening about his chest. From a very great distance he heard the miner calling anxiously to him, the voice coming through a haze of pain and weariness. Then, as things were growing black, he felt a strong hand gripping him. He was hauled forth, relieved of the weight of Hill's body. For several minutes he lay prone on the reeking floor of the tunnel. Then, in answer to the miner's frantic urging, he staggered to his feet, reeled drunkenly for a moment, steadied himself by a mighty effort of the will.

Dragging the injured man with them, they reeled and scrambled over the debris that littered the gallery floor. They had not gone far when they heard a deep and awesome rumble behind them. The walls rocked to the vibration, the supporting timbers, already strained to the utmost, creaked and groaned.

" She's let go back where yuh were, Doc," the miner gasped. " We did'nt get out a minute too soon."

After an eternity of effort they reached the main drift. A final dogged drive and they staggered from the black tunnel mouth into the bright sunlight and the blessed open air.

They laid Jim Hill down upon a plot of grass. Carson leaned over him. Hill looked up steadily to meet his gaze.

The outlaw's ashen face had undergone a subtle change; the hard lines had smoothed out; the glitter had left his eyes and they were like to the eyes of a sick child. His lips moved slightly. Carson leaned closer. Hill spoke, and his voice was different also. It was the voice of the cultured, educated man that John Ringo maintained he once had been.

" Carson," he whispered, " I'm dying—I know it. But I'm not dying in the dark. You got me out. I did you wrong,

Carson, but you returned good for evil, and, Carson, you'll not be sorry. You're what I wish I'd been, but never was— a man!"

He lay silent for a moment, his remaining hand plucking feebly at the grass blades.

"Funny," he murmured, "I never realized before how green the grass is, and how blue the sky. Always too busy raising hell, I guess."

Again he was silent. Then a last faint whisper—

"Did wrong, Carson, did wrong!"

His eyes closed, he sighed wearily, and was still.

Tom Carson straightened, and gazed down long and steadily at the dead outlaw. Yes, Jim Hill was dead, and with him died Carson's last chance to remove the cloud of suspicion that hovered over him.

But Tom Carson did not care. He had done his duty as he saw it. His conscience was clear. A great peace descended upon him. No matter what men might think of him, he stood vindicated before himself. He realized to the full the mighty and inviolable truth that at the last man must answer to himself, must pass judgment upon himself and render verdict, and from that verdict of the throned and adamant spirit, that is himself, there is no appeal!

Head held high, eyes bright, he passed down the hill to the town. Behind him, forgotten, trailed Pat Ryan, the stocky miner, who had heard every word Jim Hill uttered. Ryan's homely face was split by a grin of pleased anticipation.

When Tom Carson appeared on the street, after washing up and changing clothes, he met with a pleasant surprise. Pat Ryan, the miner, had done his work well. Prominent citizens came up to him to greet him and shake his hand and express their admiration for what he had done at the Sulphuret mine. Foremost was Mayor Thomas.

"I'm here to eat crow, Carson," the mayor said. "Uh-huh, I figger I shore owe yuh an apology for what I said to yuh a long time back. Now I got somethin' else to say. We want yore kind in Tombstone; we're goin' to need yore sort of hombre when things get goin' good again. We were all plumb damn fools not to know fust off that a feller like you couldn't be anythin' but a square shooter, no matter how funny things might look on the surface. We're proud of yuh, Carson, proud that yuh're one of us. Here's my hand on it, if yuh'll forget what's gone before and take it."

That night the bars of Tombstone were crowded with excited men who feverishly discussed the catastrophe. They spoke hopefully, optimistically. Pumping machinery would be installed. Already the Grand Central and the Contention had put in orders for steam pumps. The mines would be cleared, would soon be operating again. Prosperity, greater than ever would return. Tombstone would boom once more.

But Tom Carson knew better. He knew that no pumping machinery would ever drain the Tombstone mines. A vast subterranean lake or river had been tapped. It doubtless underlay the entire range of hills. No armour plate of steel could so sheathe the immense treasure of silver that had been the source of Tombstone's prosperity and growth. The water offered an impenetrable barrier. Tombstone was already dead, though still walking about, a galvanized corpse, whose limbs would soon stiffen.

Carson walked out into the open and pondered his future. He might remove to Tuscon or Benson, both growing towns, where his skill and experience would soon acquire him a fat practice.

But the idea was distasteful. He looked up at the blue-black sky sprangled with stars. Over the Dragoons the moon hung red. Far to the east the blue and shadowy Chiricahuas loomed against the sky. Beyond was the flat-topped mountains of New Mexico, the Pecos River, winding and shining under the stars, the wild and mysterious land of the Texas Big Bend. Great stretches. New country! New towns abuilding! Men bulking big on the trails! The Frontier!

The swinging doors of Tombstone's glittering saloons flailed back and forth as men crowded in and out. There was a clatter of talk, the thud of boot heels on the sidewalk, song and music, the click of roulette wheels, the clink of bottle necks on glass rims.

But over the Dragoons the moon hung red!

Tom Carson chuckled to himself. He turned and headed for his little office. There he set his affairs in order, assembled what he thought needful and packed his saddlebags. He got the rig on his horse, swung into the hull and squared his shoulders. Tall and lithe, the reddish moonlight etching his stern profile in flame, he rode east by south. Once he turned to gaze back at the cluster of lights on the lion's paw.

"She was a good old town," he told his horse. "I didn't lose anything by squatting there for a spell. Could still take it easy there for a while, I reckon; but I figure the easy life isn't for me. We're going to go places and do things, horse. We're going to see new places, new folks. That's what I've got a hankering for. Uh-huh, reckon I am, and always will be—just a simple Frontier doctor!"

THE END